AMONG WOLVES

JERICHO BLACK BOOK ONE

JORDAN VEZINA

MOUNTAIN WOLF PRESS

CHAPTER 1

**Der Wolf Beer Haus
Buenos Aires, Argentina.
May 5, 1975**

T he beer hall was a known gathering place not just for Germans, but for all those who had sympathized with the grand plans of Adolf Hitler. It had been identified as such more than three decades prior, and proudly retained this status even though the schemes of the mad Austrian had become ashes long ago.

Argentina (and Buenos Aires in particular)

had been a hub of Nazi activity during the Second World War and was a waypoint for many German spies. After the war, no secret was made of the fact that those who may be tried in The Hague for their actions supporting the goals of the Third Reich might find refuge in the South American country.

As a result of this, one could be excused for thinking that the atmosphere in certain Buenos Aires neighborhoods seemed almost Germanic. This is because it was. In the beginning of the movement to escape the wrath of the Allies, former Nazi Party members went underground, changed their names and even appearances. Adolf Eichmann (the architect of the Holocaust) adopted the name Ricardo Klement and sought to stay under the radar.

This proved fruitless, as he was captured by the Mossad (Israeli intelligence) on May 11th, nineteen sixty. He was then tried and executed in Israel. The former Nazi mastermind was survived by a wife and four sons.

Two of the sons decided to detach themselves from the family name, and one would even speak out against his father in later years.

The other two did not, and on May 5th, nineteen seventy-five, one sat in this very beer hall.

Klaus Eichmann held court at his private table with three of his closest lieutenants. The beer hall itself was quiet, much quieter than it had been in previous years. So much had changed.

The Eichmann brothers had also changed. Klaus thought back to the ridiculous news conference his brother Horst had held just over ten years prior, arriving to meet with the reporters dressed in a full Nazi uniform. That had been a mistake, a model of impetuous youth, full of rage and confusion, declaring that he would carry on Hitler's struggle and that his father had been guilty of no crimes.

Then the brothers had begun the attacks. Klaus and Horst formed a small Nazi cell and carried out retribution against local Jewish businesses. The message they were sending was a simple one, almost elegant in its blunt ferocity.

You are not safe.

Their private war did not last long. Their anger made them sloppy and they soon found themselves in a shootout with federal police who had raided their home. For this, Horst spent two years in prison.

After Horst was released, the brothers knew that the police would never stop watching him. Unless, of course, he was dead.

Horst Eichmann was reported dead to the Police Federal Argentina by his own brother. Supposedly he was murdered by assassins and then his body was burned in the woods. That was the story, at least. It was just what the doctor ordered if the goal was for a man to disappear, and for no one to ever look for him. There was no body to be identified, only a scorched area of forest and a pile of ashes. Some of Horst's clothing was also found burned to complete the illusion.

For over a decade Horst lived underground, with his companion Carmen Lindemann. The two did a masterful job of keeping his existence a secret, all the while networking with Nazi sympathizers around the globe and slowly building what would become a South American Fourth Reich.

It was a perfect ruse, executed with the requisite German precision. All was going perfectly until a Mossad asset on the street in

Buenos Aires snapped a photo of a poorly disguised Horst Eichmann at a roadside stand.

The front door of the beer hall opened, and a man walked in, a man who very much caught Klaus Eichmann's attention. He wasn't German, of that much Klaus was quite certain. He looked as if he may be Latin, but there was another possibility.

No, Klaus shook that thought away. Impossible. No Jew would be brazen enough to enter this place. It had always circulated in the back of his head that the Mossad may return to Argentina, and that they may specifically come for him, but it was unlikely they would march straight into Der Wolf and seize him there.

Yet, still this man was walking toward him. This man was tall, with a thin black beard and shortish black hair. It almost looked as if he had begun combing his hair that morning and then given up on it. He wore a mid-length black leather coat and button-up shirt, but none of those trivialities were what caught the eye of Klaus Eichmann the most.

What drew his eye was the long scar

crossing the man's throat. Someone had tried to kill this man and seeing as he was walking into Der Wolf Beer Haus on that warm May night, it would seem that this man had gotten the better of the exchange.

Jacob Mitzak stopped at the table of Klaus Eichmann. Their intelligence asset in the area had told them that this was where the man could be found, and he would be the surest route to locating his supposedly dead brother. The same asset had also told Jacob and the rest of the ultra-secretive Israeli intelligence unit that it would be dangerous to approach Klaus in the beer hall.

Jacob had brushed off the warning. He had killed enough Nazis to know what made them tick, and more importantly he knew what it took to stop them from ticking. Horst and Klaus Eichmann weren't even real Nazis, as far as Jacob was concerned. They were junior Nazis, and not very good ones at that.

Regardless of Jacob's personal views on the Eichmann brothers, reliable intelligence had told them that the two errant Aryans were in the process of getting ready to do something big. Saul Greenbaum (the head of Jacob's unit) had taken this intelligence to higher headquarters and been told that it was not actionable, and they were not to get involved in foreign entanglements.

Behind closed doors, Saul was given a much different directive. Locating this Horst Eichmann may lead them to a much bigger fish they had been stalking fruitlessly for decades.

So this had brought Saul Greenbaum, Jacob Mitzak, Aleks Rosen and Jane Sutcliffe to Buenos Aires on a capture or kill mission. It was most likely to be the latter. The targets were Horst and Klaus Eichmann.

Jacob pulled out a chair and sat down at the table across from Klaus Eichmann.

"This is a private table," one of Klaus' lieutenants said.

"That's okay, I'm a private man," Jacob said as he lit a cigarette. "It's a perfect fit."

Klaus smiled.

"You are... a Jew?" Klaus asked.

"Last time I checked between my legs, yes."

Klaus laughed at this.

"And a funny Jew at that!" Klaus said. "Most of you don't have a very good sense of humor, you know."

"You've been hanging out with the wrong Jews," Jacob replied.

Klaus smiled and nodded his head, attempting to take the measure of this man sitting across from him.

"Have you a name?" Klaus asked.

"I do," Jacob said.

"Then give it!" one of the lieutenants snapped.

"Jacob Mitzak," Jacob said, and sat his zippo lighter down on the table. It was the one he had taken from the first SS soldier he killed outside of the Auschwitz concentration camp. Klaus' eyes were drawn to the swastika engraved on the lighter. "But you may know me better as The Hammer Of Israel."

The room went silent.

Klaus had heard of this man. He was like a boogeyman, a myth that stalked Nazi war criminals around the world. You would hear a story about him killing a Nazi in New York, but then a week later he was in Spain. Then again in

Japan. The stories made no sense, they were clearly manufactured by the Zionists. One story had even proposed that this man went so far as to pursue a Nazi into a Soviet prison deep in Siberia.

"You... are The Hammer Of Israel?" Klaus asked, a sly smile on his face. "Is Santa Claus waiting in the car for you?"

Jacob said nothing.

Klaus tapped his finger on the table.

"As you were told, this is a private table. So, I will have to ask you to leave."

"You can ask all you want," Jacob replied. "But you will not find me to be in an obliging mood this evening."

"And why is that?" Klaus asked.

"Because I came here to complete a task, and I can't leave until said task is checked off my list."

"And what task is this?" Klaus asked.

"You."

The barmaid walked to the table and collected the empty glasses. She then set fresh beers down on the table. She was an older woman, perhaps in her late forties, but very well put together with chestnut hair and green eyes. She was what some might consider unusually fit. She held the tray in her left hand as she stood behind the larger of Klaus' lieutenants, and her hand slowly moved to her right garter.

Jacob looked up at her.

Jane Sutcliffe looked back. She had arrived a week before the rest of the team and had been carrying on the ruse of the German barmaid ever since.

Jacob nodded.

In one smooth movement she drew the baby Fairbairn knife from her garter, dropped her tray, pulled back the head of the big lieutenant and slit his throat. As if it were part of some deviously choreographed ballet, she spun around and slammed the same knife into the chest of a second lieutenant.

The first man had stumbled to the ground, clutching at his throat as blood poured from it and across the aged wood planks of the floor, but to no avail. His story was over.

In the midst of this action Jacob had already drawn his own KA-BAR knife and killed the third lieutenant.

The entire attack only lasted five seconds.

Jacob handed Jane her pistol and drew his own silenced Ruger. He kept it trained on Klaus as he wiped the blade of his knife off on the man he had just killed and then slid it back into the sheath on his belt.

Jacob could see that Klaus wanted to bolt.

"Don't do it," Jacob said. "You'll be dead before you reach the door."

Klaus relaxed his body. This man was right. There was no way he could outrun the Ruger.

There were only a dozen men left in the beer hall, and they all seemed unsure what they should do. Some were loyal to the Eichmann Brothers, but others had simply come to have a beer.

"None of you have to die!" Jane called out as she surveyed the room, her Beretta 1951 gripped in her steady hand. "But if you want to meet your maker, stay standing. All who want to see the sunrise, have a seat."

All the men immediately sat down, save for one. He was a big barrel-chested fellow who looked as if he may have been a soldier in Hitler's army and clearly did not like a woman giving him orders.

"You may want to get your hearing

checked," Jane said as she drew back the hammer on her pistol.

The man understood the implied threat and took his seat.

"We're all walking out of here," Jacob said and then turned to Klaus. "All of us."

"It's quite bold," Klaus said. "Coming here to kill me."

"We're not here to kill you," Jacob said. "You have a chance here, a chance to walk away."

Klaus cocked his head to the side.

"How is that?"

"You're coordinating with a man named Jurgen Steiner. I want him."

Klaus shook his head.

"Even if I knew where this Steiner person was, which I don't-"

"I know you don't," Jacob said, cutting him off. "But Horst does."

"Ah," Klaus said. "You want me to take you to my brother. That could be challenging."

"Why is that?"

"Because he died a year ago. Everyone knows that. It's what you might call common knowledge."

Jacob reached into his pocket, retrieved a black-and-white photograph and threw it down on the table. It was a photo of Horst Eichmann, standing beside a roadside vendor.

"That was taken two weeks ago. But I believe you, Klaus. Maybe he is dead. If that's the case I have no more need of you."

Jacob raised his pistol, leveling it at Klaus.

"Wait!" Klaus said, raising his hands in front of him as if they could stop a bullet. For the first time since Jacob Mitzak had entered Der Wolf Beer Haus, Klaus Eichmann looked scared.

"Yes?" Jacob asked. "You have something to say?"

"If I take you to him, what will you do?"

"If he tells me what I want to know, he will live. You both will."

"But... the things we've done," Klaus said, not believing Jacob's offer. "No retribution?"

"I said you would live. I didn't say there would be no retribution. You will come back to Israel with us to stand trial for your crimes against the Jewish people, but the death penalty will be off the table."

"And the alternative?"

"You die face down on *that* table in front of you," Jacob said coldly.

"I see."

Jacob could tell that Klaus' mind was scrambling, trying to come up with some other option, but there was none. He looked around the room and it was clear that no one was coming to his rescue.

Klaus placed his hands on the table, slid his chair back and stood up.

"So be it," Klaus said.

Jane kept her weapon up as Jacob walked Klaus to the door. She followed, still keeping her pistol at the ready.

"It's over!" Jane snapped at them. "Your little bullshit uprising is finished. Those of you who were part of the cell, we know your names, we know where you live. We know where your children go to school. If you want to see terror, keep pushing us. We'll show you terror."

CHAPTER 2

A Mossad Safe House
Buenos Aires, Argentina
May 8, 1975

K laus Eichmann sat at the small table sipping the glass of water they had given him. This was a strange place he found himself in, and strange people he found himself in it with. Slowly he realized that he had not yet processed what was happening and that his life was over.

Those men that Jacob Mitzak and the woman (he thought her name might be Jane) had killed were his friends. One of them he had grown up with. Now they were dead, and Klaus knew that if he didn't play his cards right, he would be too.

When they arrived at the safe house, Jacob and Jane were joined by two other men, and Klaus had heard them referred to as Saul and Aleks. They were Jews like Jacob, but he didn't think Jane was. She seemed to be an American.

They wanted him to lead them to his brother Horst. Was he really going to do it, sell out his brother?

Yes. Deep inside Klaus had known that the Fourth Reich movement spearheaded by Jurgen Steiner was over, and he had known it for a long time. Horst refused to let go. Because of this, they had been planning one last strike, one last attempt to jumpstart the movement, and because of that these people had come for them.

Klaus would spend the rest of his life in an Israeli prison, this was true, but at least he would be alive.

Saul Greenbaum led Aleks Rosen and Jacob

into the next room, where they could talk privately. None had any concerns about Jane Sutcliffe being unable to control Klaus Eichmann. She was possibly the most dangerous of the group.

"You did well," Saul said, directing the compliment at Jacob. "Minimal bloodshed, and it seems he will take us to his brother."

"But we don't even know if his brother is truly alive or even has any information on Jurgen Steiner," Aleks protested.

Saul and Jacob had been hunting Jurgen Steiner for over two decades, always close but never capturing him. As a master of counter-intelligence Jurgen was a ghost that only seemed to allow someone to find him when it served to his benefit, and then he would disappear again.

Jacob shot Aleks a disapproving look. It was no secret that Aleks did not want to be on this job, or any job really. He just needed his resume stamped with a secret mission so he could move up the ranks at Mossad headquarters.

"Be that as it may," Saul said. "We were out of options. This is the first solid lead we've had on Jurgen Steiner in years. All signs say he's about to do something big, something that will get him noticed again. We need to ensure that doesn't happen."

"Horst is the connection," Jacob said. "We know he's the one who has been communicating with Steiner."

"You really think Klaus will give up his brother?" Aleks asked, obviously not convinced.

"Absolutely. They're baby Nazis. Despite all his bluster, Klaus is not a true believer. He will not die for the cause."

"Agreed," Saul said with a nod of his head. "Klaus will take us to his brother. He just has to get us past the outer wall of Horst's home and then into the house. If Horst wants to live, he'll tell us where to find Steiner or Steiner's courier."

"When do we go?" Aleks asked.

"Now," Saul said.

"No," Aleks said, shaking his head. "We need more time. We need to file a tactical plan with—"

Jacob's laughter cut him off.

"A tactical plan?" Jacob asked sarcastically.

"This is Buenos Aires, Aleks. We've been running jobs here for nearly thirty years. We don't file tactical plans."

"I think HQ would have a different opinion on that matter!" Aleks shot back.

"Jacob is right," Saul said. "This lead has an expiration date. Word is already getting around about what happened at the beer hall. We can't wait for approval. We move now."

It was clear that Aleks didn't care for this answer, but he decided to keep any further objections to himself.

The three walked out of the bedroom and back into the kitchen. Jane was sitting in her chair across from Klaus, her Beretta laid across her lap. She looked like she was ready to kill him, regardless of what they decided.

"You'll take us to your brother?" Saul asked.

Klaus looked up at the short, powerfully built man.

"He gets the same deal I have?" Klaus asked. "No death penalty?"

Saul nodded.

"Okay," Klaus said. "I can do it. I can take you to him."

Jacob caught Jane's eye and indicated that he wanted to see her outside. She stood up from the table and passed her weapon to Aleks. She was still wearing the German barmaid's uniform, and there was nowhere to hide the pistol.

Jacob stepped out into the warm Buenos Aires evening. He looked at this watch. It was nearly two in the morning, not really the evening anymore. He felt the first sensation of fatigue behind his eyes but knew that sleep was nowhere in his future. If they could get to Horst through his brother that would launch them directly into another mission.

Jane walked out the door behind him and shut it.

Jacob took out a cigarette and lit it in the darkness. The safe house was outside of the city, and only a mile away from the field where they had parked the prop plane they had taken in. The city lights were far away, and the darkness was pervasive. It felt like it could eat into a man's bones.

"No problems getting in?" Jacob asked.

"No," Jane replied. "I still have an American passport, and I'm not wanted by Interpol."

Jacob shook his head.

"You'll have to take care of that at some point," Jane said, taking the cigarette from his hand and inhaling deeply. "You just have to get Mossad to explain that you were on a mission."

"I wasn't on a mission."

"Please, like they've never told a lie before."

"You know I'm persona non grata back there. Saul had to call in some serious favors just to get me on this job."

"How does it feel?"

"What?" Jacob asked.

"Being on a job again?"

"I was starting to like being a mercenary."

"Bullshit," Jane said. "You know you want back in. That's why you came on this job, right?"

Jacob thought about if for a moment.

"I honestly don't know anymore." He took his cigarette back, the ember glowing in the darkness. "I heard you have some fresh blood back at The Box."

"One guy," Jane said. "His name is Betz,

Betz Felman. He's an American ex-pat. Kind of reminds me of Martel Schweiz."

Jacob smiled at the memory of the former Nazi-Doctor who had helped them all those years ago in New York.

"He was a good man," Jacob said. "All the more reason to hunt down the son of a bitch who murdered him."

"I feel good about this one," Jane replied. "I know we've hit a lot of dead ends, but something about this one... it feels real. I feel like we might actually get Steiner this time."

Jacob looked at her and smiled.

"Is this the new uniform?" he asked, gesturing to the low-cut blouse and short skirt.

"Keep it up," Jane said. "See what happens."

Jacob's face turned serious.

"How is she?"

Jane shook her head.

"She'd like to see her father."

"You know why I can't. Your mother is still..."

"Being her only parent?" Jane asked, recognizing she was just as guilty of neglecting their daughter as Jacob was.

"She's twenty now, right?" Jacob asked.

"Yes. She's at NYU. Theoretical mathematics."

"She didn't get that from me, that's for sure," Jacob said.

Jane wasn't sure what to say.

"She'll understand," Jacob assured her as he dropped his cigarette to the ground and stamped it out. "Someday, when she's older. She'll understand."

"No, she won't," Jane said. "I know, because I never did."

Saul walked to the corner of the living room where Aleks stood and spoke quietly to the man.

"I know you don't want to be here," Saul said.

"What gave you that idea?" Aleks asked, sounding indignant.

"I've been doing this a long time, Aleks," Saul said, and then pointed a finger at him. "And I've known you a long time. You're not one to get your hands dirty."

"Saul, I—"

Saul held up a hand to silence him.

"It's not an accusation, just a statement of fact, and I don't hold it against you. All I ask is that you be where we ask you to be, when you are supposed to be there. We will take care of the rest."

"Of course."

Saul studied Aleks for a moment and then nodded.

The Home Of Horst Eichmann
Buenos Aires, Argentina
May 8, 1975

Jane sat in the old Studebaker with Aleks Rosen, watching as Jacob, Saul and Klaus walked to the house on the other side of the street. She wasn't happy about being relegated to a lookout, but she understood. Sending in more than two people with Klaus would draw too much attention, and obviously those two people had to be Saul and Jacob.

She also understood that she was lucky just to be on this job. She had been running missions in Jordan and Syria for the past six months and was long overdue to be pulled from active status, but she kept dodging the requests to stand down. She didn't want to. She wanted to keep going. So, when she crossed paths with Saul at Box Headquarters and he told her he needed an advance party for a job in Argentina, she jumped at the opportunity. There were only three reasons to go to Argentina: Tango, steak and Nazis.

"Don't you think this is a little... rushed?" Aleks asked from the backseat.

Jane looked at him in the rearview mirror.

"Everyone is clear on your feelings about the mission," Jane said.

"I don't have a problem with the mission," Aleks shot back. "It just seems to be moving a little fast is all."

Jane shook her head.

"That's how this works, Aleks. We move fast. Intelligence value degrades with every passing hour. You know that. You also know that Saul knows what he's doing."

Aleks decided not to respond and instead

turned and watched as the three men moved to the exterior gate of the house.

Jacob, Saul and Klaus stopped at the exterior gate. The house was quiet, as one would expect it to be at three in the morning. Particularly if it were only inhabited by a single woman still in mourning over the loss of her lover, which was the front Carmen had maintained for all of those years.

Saul looked to the call bell and then to Klaus.

"When we ring the bell, she'll come out. Call to her, get her to come to the gate," Saul said.

Jacob tapped his silenced Ruger against his arm.

"If you try anything, try to warn her, we'll leave you in the street for the dogs," Jacob said. "Understand?"

Klaus nodded.

"The words, Klaus," Jacob said. "I need to hear the words."

Klaus seemed to hesitate for a moment.

"I understand."

"Good."

Jacob reached out and rang the call bell.

A moment later a light came on in the house. They heard the front door unlatch. Klaus stood in front of the exterior wall gate, with Jacob and Saul on either side of him. They were hidden by the exterior wall itself.

"Who is it?" a woman's voice called out. "Who is there?"

"Carmen!" Klaus called out. He was careful not to shout but spoke loudly enough that she would hear him across the fifty feet of the inner courtyard. "It's Klaus!"

"Klaus?" she asked uncertainly. "What are you doing here at this hour?"

"I need to speak with him!" Klaus replied.

Carmen said nothing.

"Carmen, something has happened! Something terrible! We need to move him!"

Still no reply. Klaus could hear his own heart beating in the night's silence. Then he heard something else. The sound of bare feet on cobblestones. It was Carmen.

She moved quietly across the courtyard and stopped a safe distance from the gate, far enough away that if someone were to reach through the bars of the gate, they could not be able to grab her. She had been playing this game of secrecy for over a decade and was no amateur.

She still did not trust Klaus, she never had. He did not seem committed to the cause in the same way that his brother Horst was. He seemed like a man who could easily be broken, who could easily become that weak link in the chain which causes everything to fall apart.

"You're alone?" Carmen asked, looking back and forth down the street.

"Of course," Klaus said with a smile. "Who would be with me?"

Carmen felt the hairs on the back of her neck stand up. Something was wrong. Klaus didn't like her. Why was he smiling? He was nervous.

Carmen took a step back.

Jacob heard the footstep, a footstep that was going in the wrong direction. He stepped out of the shadows, silenced pistol raised and a finger to his lips.

Carmen froze.

"Please believe me," Jacob whispered. "I will kill you."

Carmen locked eyes with this tall man with the black beard and Ruger pistol. She saw it in his eyes. He would kill her.

"I believe you," she replied.

"Move to the gate," Jacob said.

Carmen stepped forward until she was at the gate.

"Good. You're going to be okay, Carmen. You're going to make it out of this."

Carmen nodded.

"Open the gate," Jacob said.

There was no hesitation. Carmen was committed to the cause, but she wasn't willing to die for it. She opened the gate, and Jacob, Saul and Klaus entered the courtyard.

"Where is Horst?" Jacob asked.

"In bed," Carmen replied. "Passed out. He drank too much."

"You're quite certain?" Saul asked.

"I had to check his pulse. He's practically in a coma."

Jacob stayed close to Carmen as they entered the front door of the house, his pistol at the ready. He didn't trust this woman for a moment.

The house was quiet.

Jacob stopped. It was too quiet. Drunk people snore.

The lights came on and Jacob caught the shape of a man out of the corner of his eye. He pivoted to his left, weapon up.

"Don't do it," a deep voice called out. It was Horst Eichmann.

Jacob looked at the man. He was standing in his robe, wearing a full beard and holding a silenced Ruger, the same weapon Jacob carried.

"Horst!" Klaus exclaimed. "Brother, I'm sorry! I didn't have a choice! They killed Heinrich, Adam and Wilhelm at the beer hall!"

"I told you to stop spending so much time there," Horst said, looking at his brother. He kept his weapon trained on Jacob Mitzak.

"It's not my fault. How could I have known?" Klaus protested.

"It's never your fault, Klaus, is it?" Horst asked. "Father was right about you."

"What?" Klaus asked, confused.

"Ever since that first fight at the playground. When I had to pull the other boy off you because you rolled over and let him get on your back. That day, father told me you were weak. This world we're trying to build, it doesn't have room in it for weak men, for men who would betray their own brother."

There was a wetness in Klaus' eyes. Jacob saw it.

"No," Jacob gasped.

Horst turned his weapon on Klaus and fired twice, hitting center mass. Carmen screamed. Klaus collapsed to the floor. Horst dropped his weapon and put his hands behind his head.

Jacob moved across the room and shoved Horst to the floor, pulling his hands behind his back and tying them quickly. He pulled Horst to his feet and slammed him against the wall.

"Why did you do that?" Jacob demanded.

"We're just cogs in a machine, and some are less important than others. My brother was an unimportant cog."

"Here is how this works," Saul said. Horst and Carmen were both secured to wooden chairs in the center of the room. "You're in communication with Jurgen Steiner, we know you are. You lead us to him, and you can live."

"I don't care about my life," Horst said, stone faced. "And as for this— what did you say his name was? Jordan Stoner?"

"Jurgen Steiner," Saul said.

"I have no idea what you're talking about. So you might as well kill me."

Jacob pressed the barrel of his weapon to Carmen's temple.

"And her?" Saul asked. "Do you care about her life?"

Horst turned to Carmen. She was in tears, trembling.

"I'm sorry, my love." He turned back to Saul. "Kill her if you feel you need to, it won't change the fact that I don't know what you're talking about."

Jacob looked to Saul. Saul shook his head. Jacob lowered his weapon. Carmen let out a breath.

Saul knew the gambit was pointless. Horst may have thought he loved this woman, but his love apparently had limits.

"And them?" Saul asked, holding out a

photograph of two children standing in front of a school. "Shall we kill them too?"

Horst's face went grey.

"They're just children," Horst whispered.

"Your children. Children that believe you to be dead," Saul replied. "But we won't kill them, if that's what you're worried about." Horst visibly relaxed. "We'll kill you and your former wife in front of them. Think about it, Horst. If we Jews are really what you have said you believe us to be, you must know that we do not have limits. I'm guessing, however, that you do."

Horst seemed to think about this for a moment and then nodded.

Carmen stared at him, eyes wide.

"You son of a bitch," she hissed.

"They are my children!" Horst snapped.

"And what am I?" Carmen demanded.

"Enough!" Jacob snapped. "Now isn't the time."

Jacob holstered his Ruger and retrieved his KA-BAR knife, which he used to cut Carmen loose. He pulled her to her feet.

"Remember that I said you're going to make it through this?" Jacob asked, looking into her tear-filled eyes. Carmen nodded. "For that to happen, I need you to hold it together."

As Jacob turned to cut Horst loose, Carmen watched the motion of his jacket and the way it caught against his holster.

She stepped forward, drew the Ruger from Jacob's holster, raised it and fired a single shot into Horst Eichmann's head.

His head snapped back and then his body slumped forward in the chair.

"No!" Jacob shouted. He turned, snatched the pistol out of Carmen's hand and slapped her hard across the face, hard enough that it knocked her to the floor. "Do you know what you've done?"

"He broke my heart," Carmen said quietly. "And now he has reaped the whirlwind because of it."

"We needed him," Saul said, the exasperation in his voice clear. "God dammit we needed him."

"No, you don't," Carmen said as she stood up. "Because I know where Jurgen Steiner's courier is. I know because I was Horst's courier. I was the only one who ever met with him."

CHAPTER 3

The Home of Horst Eichmann
Buenos Aires, Argentina
May 8, 1975

The four of them sat around the kitchen table in the early morning hours. Jane had stayed in the vehicle despite a strong protest that she should be included in the mission planning. The bottom line was that despite Aleks Rosen's many failings when it came to fieldwork, he was an excellent strategist. He had a unique ability to see a myriad of chess pieces in his head, keep them all organized and carry them through to execution.

"He's here," Carmen said, and tapped her finger on an intersection on French Street. "It's a boarding house. He stays on the third floor. Room thirteen."

"What's security like?" Aleks asked.

"There is none," Carmen replied. "Buenos Aires is, you know... friendly. Maybe not like it used to be, but particularly when the government put its foot down after you came for poppa—"

"Poppa?" Jacob asked.

"Adolf," Carmen said. "We called him Poppa. After the government stood up to you, we didn't think you would do it again."

Jacob looked at Saul. They were both thinking the same thing. This was too easy.

"You'll take us there," Saul said. "Specifically, you'll take Jacob there."

"Why?" Carmen asked, seeming confused. "I've shown you where it is, told you what you need to know. Why should I go?"

"Do you think you'll be safe here?" Aleks asked. "After what you've done? You killed Horst Eichmann!"

Carmen looked at Aleks for a moment and then her shoulders fell.

"No."

"We can get you out of the country."

"Paris," Carmen said. "I want to go to Paris."

"Would you like a pony while we're at it?" Jacob asked mockingly.

"Do you want him or not?" Carmen asked sharply. She knew that she was holding all the cards.

Aleks held up a hand.

"Paris it is. We have a good relationship with the Parisian government. We'll get you there and get you set up, but you'll have to wait a week or two. We can't put something like that together overnight."

"Why should I trust you?" Carmen asked.

"Because you have us over the proverbial barrel," Aleks explained. "You're right. We aren't supposed to be here. If you go talking, it creates a lot of problems, and despite what you may think, we are not wonton murderers. Everything that happened tonight is just speculation, until you step forward and corroborate it."

"I see," Carmen said.

"Remember," Aleks said. "Aside from killing Horst, you haven't actually done anything wrong. Your greatest sin is choosing your lover poorly and passing a few messages. If you play those cards you're holding the right way, in a few weeks you'll be watching the sun rise on the Chance De Lise."

Carmen couldn't help but smile at that.

Both Saul and Jacob may not have cared for Aleks, but neither man could deny that this was where he really shined. He could talk anyone into nearly anything.

"Fine," she said. "I will take you to him."

"Excellent," Aleks said with his trademark broad smile.

"May I use the restroom?" Carmen asked.

Aleks looked around and then saw the door for the bathroom in the hallway. He nodded to Jacob, who got up and went to check it. It wouldn't do for Carmen to enter the bathroom and then emerge with a shotgun.

"We have to check, you understand?" Aleks asked.

"Of course," Carmen said.

Jacob returned from the bathroom and gave the all clear.

Carmen stood up and walked to the bathroom. She entered and closed the door.

"Are we really going to let her walk?" Jacob asked, once he was sure she was out of earshot.

"Yes, we are," Aleks replied quickly.

"She's complicit!" Jacob snapped, careful to keep his voice quiet.

"See, this is the problem with you two. You've been in the field too long. This is how things work in the real world. You have to give if you want to get. I think a flat in Paris is a pretty small price to pay if we can net Jurgen Steiner."

Jacob looked at Saul.

"He's right," Saul acquiesced. "It's a good deal."

Carmen quietly closed the bathroom door. She waited for a moment. She could hear that they were talking but couldn't make out what they were saying.

She moved to a cabinet and opened the top

door. Inside was a phone, sitting behind a stack of towels.

Horst had become very paranoid about his health as he grew older, being particularly concerned about having a heart attack. Because of this there was a phone in every room of the house, even in the bathroom, in case he needed to call for an ambulance. This was highly unusual in Argentina where many people still did not have phones at all, so there was no reason Jacob Mitzak would have thought to look for it behind the towels.

Carmen quietly lifted the handset, and very slowly began dialing a number. Every turn of the rotary dial sounded like thunder and she felt that at any moment the tall bearded Jew they called Jacob would come crashing into the bathroom.

He didn't. The line connected.

"Pass a message," she whispered. "Get out."

Carmen emerged from the bathroom and returned to the kitchen table. They didn't know. They hadn't heard her, and any moment one of Ricardo's little street urchin's would be making his way to the boarding house on French Street to tip off Jurgen Steiner's courier, Roland Federov.

Perhaps she could have her cake and eat it too after all.

"When do we leave?" Carmen asked.

"Five minutes," Aleks replied.

"So soon?" she asked.

"Not my preference either," Aleks said. "But we need to get to the boarding house before dawn, so we don't lose this man."

Saul walked to the phone in the kitchen and began dialing a number.

"I'll launch from here," Jacob said, and then traced a line with his finger across the map. "Fifteen minutes from that time you will meet me here with the car."

"Understood," Aleks replied.

"You need to be there," Jacob said, locking eyes with the man. "Don't leave me with my ass hanging out in the breeze."

"I'll be there," Aleks said, sounding more than slightly annoyed.

Jacob held his gaze for a moment more and then looked over his shoulder. Saul seemed to be having quite an animated conversation with whoever was on the other end of the line. Finally, he slammed the phone down.

"What is it?" Jacob asked.

"We're blown," Saul said. "They know we're here."

"Who?" Aleks asked.

"Everyone. I don't know what happened, but the PFA were tipped off.

"We have to abort!" Aleks said. "We have to get back to the plane, right away!"

"No, we can still make it," Jacob said. "If we leave right now."

"Are you insane?" Aleks asked, his eyes wide. "We'll be caught! Or worse!"

Jacob grabbed Aleks by his collar, picked him up and slammed him against the wall.

"I came here to get Steiner!" Jacob snapped. "We have our first real lead in years, and you want to run like a coward?"

Aleks shoved Jacob away and straightened his shirt out.

"Don't touch me!"

"Stop it!" Saul shouted. "I am the commander in the field. Not you. We're doing the grab. Now get out to the car."

. . .

Jane Sutcliffe watched as the three men emerged from the house with Carmen Lindemann. What was going on? Where was Klaus? Where was Horst?

"Change of plans," Jacob said as they crossed the street to the Studebaker. "PFA is onto us. We're hitting the target now."

"Where is it?" Jane asked as she got behind the wheel and the others squeezed into the car.

"French Street, but you're not going."

"The hell I'm not!" Jane snapped.

"He's right," Saul cut in. "You've already done what you were supposed to. You supported us in the acquisition of Klaus Eichmann, and you did an amazing job, Jane. But now we need you to extract Carmen from the country."

Jane glared at Carmen. She knew who this woman was, and who she had been sleeping with. She wanted to continue her tirade, but she trusted Saul. If he needed her to do this, it was important.

"I'm leaving tonight?" Carmen asked.

"Yes," Saul replied. "Jane will take you across the border where you'll wait until we get word that Paris is set up. But if anything happens to us, Jane will put a bullet behind your ear, and don't think for a moment that just because you're a woman she won't do it."

"Killing women is my specialty," Jane said quietly as she started the engine.

They had returned to the small safe house where a second vehicle was stored. Jane secured Carmen in the passenger seat and then returned to the Studebaker. They had originally wanted to take Carmen to the target house but decided against it. Trying to manage her while they were attempting to apprehend the courier would be too many moving pieces.

Jane leaned in the window.

"You know that I wish I was coming with you," Jane said.

"What you're doing now is important," Saul assured her. "And we'll see you back in the desert."

Jane looked to Jacob.

"What about you," she asked. "Will I see you? Are you coming back into the fold?"

"That depends. Will you be wearing that German barmaid outfit?" Jacob asked.

Jane extended her middle finger in response.

The last stop for the group before hitting the house was the field where the prop plane was parked. Saul would ready it for extraction, hopefully with one more passenger. Carmen had given them all the information they would need to apprehend this Roland Federov and get him out of the country for interrogation.

Originally, the plan had been to question him at the safe house, but since half the country seemed to know that they were there, that idea was now off the table.

"This won't be easy," Saul said. "If you get there and anything looks wrong or you see too many police around you abort. Do you understand?"

"Yes," Jacob replied.

"No cowboy stuff."

"Are there any Jewish cowboys?" Jacob asked with a smile.

"Levi Strauss," Aleks interjected. "He was Jewish."

Jacob and Saul both looked at Aleks quizzically.

"Why do you know that?" Jacob asked.

Aleks shrugged.

"I know things."

A Boarding House on French Street
Buenos Aires, Argentina
May 8, 1975

Roland "Rollo" Federov woke in the pre-dawn darkness to feel the ocean breeze blowing across his face. It was a surreal feeling, and he didn't open his eyes at first, once again concerned that it may be a dream. There had been no ocean breeze blowing through the windows in Kolyma Prison, and most certainly not the privacy he was afforded at this house on French Street. It wasn't much, but he had a private room and a washbasin to clean himself. Such simple things, but they were luxuries he had not known in quite some time.

That was the story of Kolyma. Filthy conditions, freezing temperatures and herded into cages like rats. Rollo didn't know much about what the future held for him, but he did know that Kolyma Prison in the Siberian region of the Soviet Union was a place he would never return. He would dictate his own destiny by biting down on the barrel of a gun before he allowed that to happen.

Buenos Aires, on the other hand, was very much to his liking, and he thought it a pity that he would not be able to stay longer. The women, in particular, were very much to his liking. Even if none of them would be fit to take as a wife.

Rollo stood up from the ancient bed with its sagging mattress, and stretched out his five foot eight, two-hundred-pound frame. The man was built like a boxer, with close-cropped hair and a face hardened by time and in possession of a jaw you could hang a lantern on. Tattoos earned in the various prisons he had been sent to throughout his life adorned his body, to include an eagle gripping a swastika on his right bicep. In retrospect this one had not been a very good decision as it made it difficult for him to walk freely in some places wearing short sleeves, but Rollo also did not believe in trying to hide who he was.

At five in the morning the boarding house was quiet, and one could only hear the footsteps of the dock workers leaving the building and the rats who never departed, the same ones that would begin to gnaw on a person's toes in the dark of the night if they slept without their boots on.

Rollo walked to the washbasin and ladled some water into it, followed by a ladle into his mouth. It wasn't the best tasting water, but it served to quench the dryness of a throat that had become intimate with too many cervezas the night before. That was another vote in Argentina's favor; they made very good beer. It was also a place where people like Rollo could move freely. It was not quite as permissive an environment for some Nazi war criminals as it used to be but was still a useful meeting place. That was why Jurgen Steiner had chosen it to point Rollo toward his final destination.

Jurgen was one of the aforementioned Nazi war criminals, and Rollo had met the man in Kolyma. Since then they had maintained a close relationship, and Jurgen served as something of a mentor to the young man. Before Kolyma, Rollo had been nothing more than unfocused rage housed in a resilient shell. Jurgen took that fire and used it to forge the operative he needed, a man who could help him deliver his message to the United States: *You are not safe.*

This took Rollo to Buenos Aires, to make final arrangements and then travel to Mexico where he would retrieve a crate buried in the desert. It was quite clever (Rollo thought) how Jurgen had set all of this up. No single man knew the big picture, or where all the skeletons were buried. Each of them received only one piece, the piece that was relevant to him or her. That way, if any of them were captured they would be unable to reveal the entire plan.

Rollo stepped to the doorway and looked out the small peephole into the dark hallway. There was no one. It was empty as it should be at that time of the morning.

Rollo jumped a little as he heard the knock at the door. He could not see anyone through the peephole. Stepping back, he reached into his waistband for the .38 pistol and pulled the door open as he drew it. The small boy standing in the hallway seemed to take no note of the weapon, and perhaps it was not the first time a gun had been pointed at him.

Of course, Rollo had not seen him because of his height.

The boy held out a single slip of paper for Rollo, a message he was apparently supposed to deliver. No sooner had Rollo taken the message than the boy sprinted away, laughing as he bounded down the stairs. Rollo turned over the small slip of paper and read it.

Get out.

Jacob Mitzak ran as fast as his feet would carry him down the narrow stone alley that led to French Street.

The streets of Buenos Aires were already buzzing at five in the morning as Jacob leapt over a pile of discarded bicycles and emerged onto French Street. A quick pivot to the right and he saw the boarding house where he would find Roland Federov, the man who would lead them to Nazi mastermind Jurgen Steiner. Normally they would surveil a target like this for at least twenty-four hours, but that was off the table. Instead, Jacob was just going to hit the third floor, kick the door in and give the neo-Nazi the good news.

Unfortunately, the PFA had other plans. Jacob had been so focused on the boarding house he didn't notice the group of three police officers to his left when he emerged from the alley and turned to the right. The first man tackled him and were it not for Jacob's height the police officer would have taken him down. Instead, Jacob stepped to a forty-five-degree angle with his left foot and threw the man over his shoulder using his hips. The impact of the man hitting the pavement was enough to knock the wind out of him and give Jacob the time he needed to draw his Ruger and turn to face the two remaining policemen.

Both men froze, hands hovering over their weapons.

"Whatever they're paying you, it isn't enough," Jacob said in Spanish.

The men hesitated for a moment, as if they may still have some fight in them, but then thought better of it and turned and ran.

. . .

The boarding house was dark, and Jacob thought it was darker than it should have been. He ran up the steps past the ancient light fixtures, and more than once wondered if one of his feet would break through the rotting floorboards. The place smelled like death.

One by one Jacob Mitzak began kicking doors in, going room to room looking for his quarry. At least he knew that Federov would stand out like a sore thumb. A Russian neo-Nazi with a crew cut and built like a fireplug didn't exactly blend in.

Halfway down the hallway Jacob heard a loud thump against one of the doors and throwing his shoulder into it met resistance. It wasn't the lock stopping him because the door was open a crack. Something was pushed up against it. This was the one. Federov was escaping.

Rollo had shoved the bed against the door when he started hearing the crashes from the hallway, and understood that someone was going room to room, almost certainly looking for him. Jurgen told him that the Israelis may have been in Argentina looking for the former SS commander, and that if they somehow discovered that Rollo was linked to him, they may come for him as well.

Sure enough, just a moment after Rollo wedged the ancient metal bed frame between the door and the washstand that was bolted into the wall, whoever was in the hallway attempted to get in his door. The hasty barricade would hold, but not forever.

Rollo threw his knapsack over his shoulder and pulled the window open, looking down at the rusted fire escape that would take him three stories to the street below. Quickly but carefully he slid out onto the landing and began his descent.

Jacob heard a loud metal creaking coming from inside the room and stopped his assault on the blocked door. It was the fire escape. Without hesitation Jacob bolted back down the stairs, frantically racing to street level. He could not lose Federov. That would be a disaster.

Traffic on the street seemed to have almost doubled since Jacob first entered the building, and he negotiated his way past a dozen people before he rounded the corner of the building in time to see Rollo hit the ground and run down an alleyway.

Jacob turned to follow and felt himself being tackled again, just like in the boarding house but this time it was more than one man. There were at least five policemen, and two of them had just taken him to the ground. There was no time to treat them with kid gloves, and Saul had confirmed that the PFA were under direct orders to assassinate them.

Reaching to his boot Jacob retrieved the KA-BAR knife stashed there, and first used the end of the handle to deliver quick strikes to the ribs of the men trying to wrestle with him. They were obviously amateurs and had not transitioned to their clubs or guns. That was a mistake The Hammer of Israel never made.

After receiving a hard strike to the ribs, the average man will quickly lose his will to fight, and these men were no different. They quickly moved back from their intended victim and began clumsily reaching for their guns, but before they could clear their holsters Jacob already had his Ruger out and pointed at them.

"Drop your weapons now!" Jacob shouted. While he was not about to put his life on the line to avoid killing these men, he knew they were just pawns, and he would avoid shooting them if possible. "On the ground! Do it!"

The policemen froze. There were five of them, but something about this man told them that if they chose to gamble, Jacob Mitzak would be the one with the ace up his sleeve. Each officer dropped his weapon, and they began to get down on the pavement.

Jacob looked over his shoulder, but it was too late. Federov was gone. He had lost him.

Moving quickly, Jacob kicked the dropped guns away and moved backward from the policemen when he heard the wailing of sirens in the distance, and then he saw them. It looked like a virtual army racing toward him, a mix of PFA officers and what looked like soldiers. This was quickly going from bad to worse, but he knew he only had two blocks to the rendezvous point with Aleks Rosen.

With no further delay, Jacob turned and broke into a dead sprint down the main street. Fortunately, the crowd had thinned, as the Argentinians wanted nothing to do with a police or military action, and Jacob shared their opinion.

Only one block to go, and he could feel the sweat covering his body, his heart pounding and his vision blurring as he ran harder than he ever had; perhaps the only exception being his escape into the woods from Auschwitz.

A moment later Jacob broke out onto Avenue Santa Fe and saw Aleks' car. More specifically, he saw it driving away.

"Son of a bitch!" Jacob snapped and turning to his left began to re-route his escape.

"I lost him," Aleks said, walking to the plane where it was parked in a clearing in the field.

"What do you mean you lost him?" Saul shouted.

"There were just too many! Police and military were both closing in. They would have barricaded the streets, we weren't going to be able to get away in a car," Aleks explained. "He's resourceful, he'll come up with something."

"You had better hope so," Saul said, glaring at the man.

Aleks began preparations to get the plane airborne while Saul stowed their gear in the small cabin. The prop plane was barely big enough for the three of them and their equipment, but each time they required its use they somehow made it work.

Having finished with his load out, Saul stepped back down from the plane and walked into the field. He stood motionless, watching the road that they had parked a safe distance away from. It wasn't very well traveled, and it would be a safe bet that any vehicle heading toward them would either be Jacob Mitzak or the Police Federal Argentina.

"We have to go!" Aleks called out.

"We wait," Saul replied.

Aleks wanted to continue pushing the issue, but instead tried a different tactic.

"How long?" Aleks asked. "This mission isn't over, Saul. We may have lost Federov but we still have other options. If we're caught here though, we're finished. Maybe the Mossad as well. It hasn't really been that long since Eichmann."

Saul turned to look at Aleks. He would like to have thought the younger man was being dramatic, but he knew that he wasn't. After the covert operation to capture Adolf Eichmann fifteen years earlier, diplomatic relations between Argentina and Israel had become strained, to say the least. It was only in recent years that those relations were finally improving. If Mossad agents were captured in Argentina once again trying to capture a foreign agent? It would be disastrous. It could be the type of event that ends an intelligence agency.

"We owe him a little more time."

"I ask again, how much?" Aleks insisted.

Saul's head snapped to the left, toward the sound of a single motorcycle engine. The sun was not yet up, but Saul could see a single headlight on the road. He knew that it was Jacob.

Saul smiled.

"Looks like he made it after all."

Jacob Mitzak pulled up to the plane and leapt off of the motorcycle before it had even stopped rolling. Without breaking his stride, he walked toward Aleks Rosen. Aleks could see the anger in the man's eyes and held up a hand. He knew what was coming.

"Wait! Jacob, I stayed as long as I-"

Jacob Mitzak's right fist connected squarely with Aleks' nose, knocking the man back off of his feet and to the ground. Saul lunged forward between the two and grabbing Jacob in a bear hug spun the man around, away from his intended target.

"Jacob! Stop it! We don't have time for this!" Saul shouted.

"I had five more minutes!" Jacob shouted. "You should have been there!"

"I think you broke my nose!" Aleks shouted, holding it as he stood up.

In the distance they heard the sound of sirens.

"They weren't that far behind me," Jacob said. "We have to go."

Port Of Buenos Aires
Buenos Aires, Argentina
May 8, 1975

Roland "Rollo" Federov walked down the long pathway that lead him toward the container ship he would take to Mexico. Once he was there, he would find the crate that had been buried in the desert and meet his connection. He still could not believe what he had been told by Jurgen Steiner.

Americans. His coconspirators would be American college students. Rollo had heard a lot of strange stories about Americans with communist or socialist leanings, but he still found it hard to believe that they would help him with this task.

Until he met the girl. She had traveled to Buenos Aires a week prior and met with him. She was a mad dog. A beautiful, mad dog. Rollo had to admit (if only to himself) that he was quite taken with her. He didn't know about her compatriots, but he knew that she was a true believer. She would do what she said she would. She could be relied upon in the struggle that was coming.

That ocean wind hit his face again, and he smiled. At least, he smiled as much as he ever allowed himself to.

"You're early."

Rollo turned to see Heinrich Weber, Jurgen's right hand standing beside a pylon. Rollo didn't care for the old Nazi, but he respected him. His appearance was always a little jarring, considering his prosthetic nose.

"Someone came for me, at the boarding house," Rollo replied. "I'm not sure who it was, but I think they knew who I was."

Heinrich looked around.

"Well, it seems you absconded quite nicely."

Rollo looked at him quizzically.

Heinrich sighed.

"Got away, Rollo. You got away."

Rollo understood.

"Yes, I did. But not without some effort."

Heinrich handed Rollo a thick envelope which the Russian then opened. Inside were some forged identity documents, thick bundles of cash and a map.

"Will I see you there?" Rollo asked. "In San Francisco?"

"No," Heinrich replied. "My duties are calling me elsewhere."

"East Germany?" Rollo asked.

Heinrich nodded.

"I'd like to go someday. See what it's like. I think it would suit me."

"I think it would," Heinrich replied. "Jurgen is coordinating with Said Al Assan in San Francisco. You'll be meeting him there soon enough."

"The Arab?" Rollo asked.

Rollo had not been pleased to find out they were aligning themselves with Arabs. He had met Said Al Assan before and found him to be agreeable, but he was still what Rollo considered to be a mongrel. At least they had a common enemy, that enemy being the Jews.

"Yes, the Arab."

Rollo nodded.

"You don't have a problem with that, do you?" Heinrich asked.

"No," Rollo replied. "The enemy of my enemy is my friend, correct?"

Heinrich smiled and nodded.

It was true, a man like Roland Federov would not have been his first choice for an intermediary, but he was reliable and seemed able to understand at least his own piece of the greater puzzle. Heinrich also knew that Jurgen had a great deal of faith in young Rollo, and that was enough for Heinrich.

If everyone just did their part, soon enough they would all be living in a much different world.

CHAPTER 4

**A Roadside Cafe
Montevideo, Uruguay
May 10, 1975**

S aul, Jacob and Aleks sat around the small table drinking coffee and scanning every available newspaper for any mention of what had happened in Buenos Aires just days before. There was nothing. No mention of the stabbings at the beer hall or the disappearance of Klaus Eichmann or Carmen Lindemann.

"Do you think they covered it up?" Aleks asked.

"It's possible," Saul replied as he laid his newspaper down. "There is no love lost between the government and the Eichmann brothers. They're better off suppressing the story than letting it raise concerns again about their sovereignty being violated. It would make them appear weak."

"Better for us that way," Jacob said. "Fewer questions to answer."

"How long do you think?" Aleks asked. "How long should we stay here before heading back?"

Mission protocol had required that they wait a while in Uruguay for things to cool off before making the longer journey back home to Israel.

Saul looked down at the paper he had been reading. It was a copy of the San Francisco Chronicle.

"Did you see this?" Saul asked, tapping an article on the second page.

Aleks looked at it. It was a story about a double murder in San Francisco that seemed to have connections to a Nazi war criminal and a Palestinian terror group.

Aleks shook his head.

"No, I hadn't seen that."

"I don't think it's a coincidence. I think it had something to do with whatever Jurgen Steiner has planned." Saul looked at the article again. "I'm interested in this boy who was involved. He could be a useful asset."

"We'll have to file a report when we get back," Aleks said. "Perhaps I can get clearance to assess any potential intelligence value."

"We're not going back," Saul said firmly and then looked to Jacob. "We're going to San Francisco. We're going to look into this."

"Saul, that totally violates operational protocols. We have to go back first and request permission."

Jacob laughed.

"Oh, I'm sorry," Aleks said. "Is that funny to you?"

"How's your nose?" Jacob asked.

"Fuck you."

"You can go back and request permission, Aleks," Saul continued. "That way once you get it we'll already be on the ground and ready to go."

"We have these protocols in place for a reason!" Aleks said insistently.

"I promise you we won't do anything until we get the all clear."

Aleks didn't like this, but he also knew that once Saul Greenbaum got an idea in his head, there would be no talking him out of it.

"Fine," Aleks said. "But not a move until you talk to me."

Jacob read the article Saul had shown them as Aleks flagged down a pedi-cab and began his journey back to Tel Aviv.

"Are we really going to?" Jacob asked. "Wait for his permission before we do anything?"

"What do you think?" Saul asked.

Jacob smiled.

"Can I count on you?" Saul asked.

"What do you mean?" Jacob replied, sounding a little hurt. "Look at what we just did. Didn't I come through?"

"It's just that you can be a little unpredictable," Saul said. "You've been out there on your own for a long time. Do you really think you're ready to come back?"

Jacob thought about it.

"I haven't always made the right moves, Saul. To be honest, I'm not even sure what I need anymore, so maybe it's best to go back to basics for a while."

"There's work in San Francisco, while we're waiting."

"Targets?" Jacob asked.

"Possibly," Saul replied. "I'm still waiting on confirmation."

Jacob knew what that meant. There were Nazi war criminals in San Francisco in need of killing, and he would be the one to do it.

Curtina, Uruguay
May 11, 1975

Jane had been traveling with Carmen for three days, and her feelings toward the former mistress of Horst Eichmann had not warmed in the least. She found the woman to be overly concerned with her appearance and she continued to pepper Jane with questions about her accommodations in Paris. No matter how many times Jane told her that she didn't handle that sort of thing the questions continued to come.

The bottom line was that Jane Sutcliffe did not think they should be making deals like this with people like Carmen Lindemann. Regardless of those feelings, though, she had done exactly as Saul Greenbaum asked and had gotten the woman across the border and to the small town of Curtina on Brigadier Gral Fructuosa Rivera. It was nowhere. Barely a speck on the map. No one would come looking for them there.

Jane pulled the car to a stop beside the phone booth that sat on the edge of town like a silent testament to the march of technology, even in a place like Curtina.

"What are we doing here?" Carmen asked, applying her lipstick in the rearview mirror now that the vehicle had finally stopped.

"We have to call in," Jane said. "To see about your... arrangements."

"Of course," Carmen said with a smile.

Jane stepped out of the car and Carmen followed her, always curious about how her deal was being handled.

Jane opened her bag and pulled out the sack of coins she carried for making calls back home. At least out in the middle of nowhere she wouldn't have to worry about anyone trying to listen in on the call.

She dialed a number from memory and waited for the connection to go through.

"It's Avenger 3/1," she said, giving her call-sign to the switchboard operator at Mossad headquarters. She waited for a moment. "Yes, I'm here. Yes, I have her."

Jane turned to where Carmen was standing beside her car. She reached back into her canvas bag and retrieved a small derringer pistol, which she then gripped in her right hand.

"No, it went south. I don't know," Jane said. "She was talking crazy, about how she had betrayed Horst and she couldn't live with herself."

This caught Carmen's attention. She turned from where she had been admiring her reflection in the car window and met Jane's eyes.

"She shot herself with a little pistol she must have had hidden somewhere."

Carmen's hands began to tremble and she dropped her bag.

"I couldn't stop her," Jane said as she raised the pistol. "I take full responsibility."

Carmen broke into a run, heading down the road toward the town. She only made it a dozen steps before Jane Sutcliffe hung up the phone and pulled the trigger. Carmen's head snapped forward, and then she fell to her knees and collapsed in the road.

Fisherman's Wharf
San Francisco, California
July 25, 1975

"He doesn't look like much," Jacob said as he and Saul stood across the street from the small art gallery.

Inside was a young man, tall with blonde hair. He appeared to be in his late teens or early twenties.

"Neither did you," Saul replied.

"I'm surprised you can remember back that far."

"I'm not that old," Saul countered. "Besides, we all have to start somewhere."

"What makes him so special?" Jacob asked. "What makes you so sure he'll be able to do what we're going to ask of him?"

Saul thought about this for a moment.

"We both know what he went through, the newspapers were quite thorough in their treatment of him."

"You mean the hatchet job they did on him."

"It wasn't the first time the media has tried to crucify a hero, it won't be the last," Saul said. "This young man is in a unique position. He didn't ask for any of this, and he almost certainly won't want to help us."

"So why will he?"

"For the same reason that he didn't just turn a blind eye to the evil lurking within his own family. He has a reflex at his core to do what is right, and something like that can't be taught."

"What's this kid's name again?" Jacob asked.

'Will," Saul replied. "Will Hessler."

CHAPTER 5

The Home Of Diane Hessler
San Francisco, California

"Jew! Off my lawn!"

Will Hessler stopped his painting and looked up to the window of his bedroom, the same one that afforded a view of the front yard. On the sidewalk beyond their front lawn he could see his classmate Isabelle Dyer standing, a look of shocked terror staining her face. The girl clutched her bag to her chest, frozen in place.

Isabelle had begun painting with Will,

mostly at his grandfather's house. They shared a love of watercolors and soon enough this shared interest in painting had seemed to spark something more. At least Will hoped it would. Will knew what his mother would think of this, and had hoped to avoid a meeting. She was supposed to have been at one of her social clubs, but apparently had returned home early.

"Ein Jew! Vermin! Get off my god damn lawn!" Diane shouted, her rage causing her to break into fragmented German.

Will leapt to his feet and rushed down the hallway and out the front door, brushing by his mother in the process. He never looked back at her, but could feel the sting of her last words biting into his shoulder like a rabid dog.

"Is this what you do when I am not home? Jew loving bastard! Do not come home tonight Jew lover! I will kill you too!"

Isabelle cried. She cried, shook, and finally vomited on the sidewalk as Will held her hair back. Diane Hessler had been clutching in one hand the Nazi flag that normally hung over her mantle. Now Isabelle's body was breaking down, consuming her innocence to feed her fear.

"I- I'm sorry Will," she said in-between choking sobs. "I just knocked on the door, I swear! That's all I did!"

Will sat down on the curb beside Isabelle and placed his hand on hers.

"I'm sorry Isabelle, I thought that she wasn't going to be at home."

Isabelle stared at Will through bloodshot eyes.

"You told me, I know you told me that she was like this, and that's why I shouldn't come to your house, but I never imagined. I never imagined someone could be like that."

Will looked down at the ground. He didn't know what to say. There was no excusing his mother's actions, no explaining them away.

"She's just... it's just how she is."

"That is not okay, Will! You understand that, don't you?"

"Of course!" Will said quickly, not wanting Isabelle to think that he was like his mother. "It's just that she's my mother. I don't know what to say."

"And your grandfather? He isn't like that, he's always been so kind to me."

"I'm sorry, Isabelle."

Isabelle looked at Will for a moment, and then her face softened.

"It's okay, Will. We just won't go to your mom's house anymore, but we can still be friends."

Isabelle gave Will a weak smile, but he felt nothing but guilt. If his mother had her way, Isabelle Dyer would be lying in a shallow grave covered in lime.

Will Hessler did return home, despite his mother's warning. He entered the house in the relative darkness and found her sitting in silence at the kitchen table. She was waiting for him.

Diane Hessler was thin, much thinner than she ever had been before. New lines traversed her face and the runaway streaks of gray in her hair seemed to be multiplying on a daily basis. She was still beautiful, but hardened by her hatred. The symptoms of this hardening were tearing her apart inside, cracking the veneer of her soul and sharpening the edge of her cruelty.

"You have shown me... that I am alone," Diane whispered.

"Mom, you're not alone."

"You are my son." She looked up at Will. "I gave birth to you. I will respect that, but I am alone. This fight, this... struggle is mine alone. You are not fit to stand beside me. You have proven that beyond a shadow of a doubt."

Will Hessler felt cold inside. Seventeen years old and his mother now seemed to be severing their relationship. It was also in that moment that Will realized for the first time that they had never had a real relationship to begin with because this severing of ties did not feel like it changed much. If he had ever known his father, at least there would perhaps be some balance, but that had not been his lot in life.

Will thought that he would go to his grandfather and ask the man to try to talk some sense into his daughter. In this black math equation, the Nazi war criminal Franklin Hessler was the sane one.

· · ·

Franklin stood beside the couch with his hand on his daughter's shoulder. He was a proud man, taller than average and quite fit for his sixties. Even if you knew nothing of his past, Franklin Hessler still inspired a certain degree of respect. You could easily see that this was a man used to getting his way.

"I should not have reacted the way I did," Diane said, and then her lips pressed tightly together, draining them of their color. "You know how I feel, William. You know how I feel and still you brought that girl to my home."

"Am I supposed to have only friends who qualify for the master race?" Will asked.

"Do not be insolent!" Diane snapped. "I am trying to tell you that I was wrong to act the way I did, but you must understand why I feel as I do! You may associate with the Jew girl if you must, but do not rub it in my face!"

Diane stared at her son coldly for a moment and then shook her father's hand off of her shoulder and walked out of the room.

Franklin watched his daughter depart their company and then looked to his grandson.

"Walk with me boy."

· · ·

"William, do you understand what it is I did during the war?"

"Perhaps not fully," Will replied.

It was true. Will knew the basics, that his grandfather was a nazi party officer, but not much beyond that. Perhaps on some level he had not wanted to know the full truth.

"You are becoming a man now, and I think you are old enough to know everything. It may help you better understand why your mother is the way she is." Franklin removed a cigarette case from his pocket and pulled out one of his favored Roth-Handle cigarettes. "I was in the SS-SD, special duty. We followed the invading forces on the Eastern Front and cleaned up the Jews we found, to avoid wasting the time of the ground troops who were put to better use fighting the Soviets."

"I'm not sure you need to be telling me all of this," Will said.

"It is important, Will. As I said, it may help you better understand your mother, and why she is less tolerant that I am. I have dealt with the reality of what I did. I also believe that the Jews have changed and what we put them through forged them into a different animal.

They are wiser now, and more respectful of the fury that may befall them if they attempt to supplant their betters." Franklin stopped, removed his hat and smoothed his hair down. "Those who judge us did not live through the Germany between wars. They did not feel the Jewish threat encroaching upon their bloodline. The Jews thrived in the aftermath of the first war, we were merely striking back. I grew up in the ashes of the Versailles Treaty, I remember what the Big Four did to us. It was a rape, William. A rape of the German nation that the Jews were only too happy to capitalize upon."

"The Holocaust, though. Why so many?"

"When a man attacks you with a weapon, you do not disarm him and privilege him to attack you another day. You must pummel him into submission and ensure that he cannot rise again to take your life or the lives of your loved ones. You must make the result of such an action so horrifying that he would never think of doing it again." Franklin exhaled a long line of smoke. "Now, the world is different, and the Jew is different. I understand this, but your mother does not. That is the difference between us, and why she acts as she does."

"The things I hear her say, the people she meets with…" Will seemed uncertain if he should say what was on his mind.

"Out with it," Franklin Hessler snapped.

"I think she's dangerous."

Franklin looked as if the idea had never occurred to him before.

"She is afraid, William. Her fear feeds her hate, but I do not think your mother is dangerous."

Franklin Hessler heard the ring of his front door, and set his paintbrush down, taking a moment to observe what he had been working on over the past hour. He then cleaned his hands with a turpentine rag and walked down the short hallway.

He opened the door to find a short, stocky man standing on his front step, staring at him through thick, black-framed glasses.

"Franklin Hessler?"

The man at the door spoke with a German accent and appeared to be a quite formidable looking Jew. For a moment, Franklin thought that the man might be a Nazi hunter from the

Israeli intelligence agency Mossad. Was it possible that they had somehow found him? It occurred to him that perhaps he should not have begun using his true name when they moved to the United States, but Hessler was a common German name. It had just seemed like it would not be a problem. Had he been wrong?

"That is my name."

"I am Irving Dyer," the man said and held out his hand.

Franklin Hessler shook hands with his visitor.

"Mister Dyer. Yes, you are young Isabelle's grandfather."

"Yes, I am. I should mention that it was only after several interrogations as to why she was crying that she told me if I must speak to someone that you would be the wiser choice. She did not want me to."

"That is understandable. Would you like to come in?"

"Yes, please."

Franklin Hessler hesitated, and Irving Dyer took note of this.

"Mister Dyer, I want to help. I can tell just in the short time we have known one another that I like you. However, me must agree upon one thing."

"Which is?"

"We must agree that the past and what we may have done in it is indeed past."

"Indeed."

Irving Dyer was tired of fighting. Very, very tired. His first thought upon hearing Franklin Hessler's request was that he would like to slit the old Nazi's throat then and there. He did, after all, have a singular talent for killing Nazis, one that he had honed over the course of fighting with the American army for a year in Europe, and then during a brief stint with the fledgling Center for Co-Ordination (later renamed The Mossad) hunting down Nazi war criminals in New York.

That was all behind him now. Irving had learned that if he insisted upon pursuing vengeance to the grave, that was exactly where it would put him, and much sooner than he might like.

Perhaps Franklin was right, and they did need to put the past behind them. He did, after all, seem like a nice enough man, and it was unlikely that he was some architect of the Holocaust. His story of being a simple combat officer on the Eastern Front was most likely true. Irving had heard of German soldiers fighting through the entire war without ever knowing of Adolf Hitler's supposed Final Solution.

Franklin Hessler apologized profusely for his daughter's behavior and assured Irving that it would never happen again. After that matter had been resolved, Franklin and Irving continued to talk, discussing events in post-war Germany as well as the formation of Israel.

"I don't mean to pry," Franklin said. "But where are Isabelle's parents?"

Franklin could see by the change of expression on Irving's face that the answer would not be a pleasant one.

"A drunk driver, many, many years ago. Before Isabelle was born."

"Before she was born?" Franklin asked, confused.

"My Daughter was pregnant," Irving continued. "We made the decision to save Isabelle."

"I... see," Franklin said. "Young Isabelle will be safe at my home, Irving. I promise you that."

John Kellerman was the only Inspector on the San Francisco police force with one leg. The fortunes of that leg had been decided well after the surrender of Germany. Through four years of fighting in the Pacific and Europe, John had suffered only a few scratches but lost his leg after he fell off the back of a truck and was run over by the jeep that followed it. He always said he would kick himself for being so clumsy if only he could physically do so.

It was a long and difficult process for John to graduate the police academy. Only after he outran half of the cadets and put ten rounds into the same bullet hole during his firing test did the department finally relent and allow him to become a police officer.

John thought he had seen the worst humanity had to offer during the war, but he found this not to be the case. Each day, the city of San Francisco presented him with horrors previously unimaginable, and year-after-year the horrors only seemed to grow, building toward some coming crescendo.

The new case he was working had begun as a simple hit-and-run but became something more when additional facts were uncovered.

A young man had been found on the side of the road in the Outer Sunset District. At first glance, it appeared he had been struck by a car, manslaughter to be sure, but not something that the Homicide Bureau would be straining against its leash to take a bite out of.

The problem John ran into was those additional facts. Whoever hit the young man then stopped the car to see what had happened. After that, the driver struck him in the head and left. There was also a possibility that the driver had removed an item from the victim, a Star of David that family and friends said he always wore.

John Kellerman was canvassing the neighborhood with his partner Ronald Stein. Ronald was inexperienced as an inspector but had a good nose for the unusual. Observing things that were out of place was a valuable skill for an

Inspector to have. Even if he had never been in a room before, he might notice if things were out of sorts.

Normally, canvassing a neighborhood was a function that an Inspector would have the uniformed officers perform, but on something like this Kellerman knew it would be best if he got a handle on the locals himself. SFPD uniforms were good, no doubt about it, but they weren't "poker players" as Kellerman was often heard to say. John knew that after years of detective work, you learned to read a man or a woman, and that you could gather so much more information from just the twitch of an eye than you could from a thousand words.

"You think they're making a bigger deal out of all this than it really is?" Ronald asked, sipping at his cup of steaming coffee.

Kellerman mopped some sweat off his brow with a handkerchief and then tucked it back into his pocket.

"How can you drink that in this heat?" Kellerman asked.

"It keeps me awake."

"I think it is a big deal," Kellerman said, answering Ronald's question. "It wasn't bad enough to hit the guy, he had to kick him in the head. Did you see the names on that canvas list I gave you?"

Ronald unfolded the list and looked at it for a moment.

"They're all German names."

"The guy who got hit was Jewish, and someone took his Star of David. There was no struggle, there was no cause for beating the victim after he was already hit by the car, except one," Kellerman said as he held up a finger.

"Contempt."

"Exactly. It was only after the driver realized the victim was a Jew that he kicked our boy in the head. If he hadn't been Jewish, I really think the driver would have called an ambulance."

"And he took the Star of David because..."

Kellerman shrugged.

"A memento?" He scratched his head and looked around at the houses. "Maybe this guy had wanted to kill a Jew—or just anyone for a long time and never had the balls to do it. Or maybe he's killed a lot of Jews and is in the habit of taking personal possessions off them."

"Like, a lot," Ronald said, understanding.

"Yeah. Hell, if I'm right we might even end up calling Interpol or the Mossad on this one."

"Mossad?"

"Israeli Intelligence. They like going into other countries and removing certain articles. Personal articles."

"Like Nazi war criminals."

"What's the next name on that list?"

Ronald looked it over and nodded to a house across the street.

"Guy named Hessler."

"Kraut name if I ever heard one."

Irving Dyer had already left when the policemen came to Franklin Hessler's doorway. They were very polite and came inside when Franklin invited them for a cup of coffee. Kellerman declined, but Ronald Stein happily took a cup of the thick Turkish concoction.

"I certainly am having a lot of visitors today." Franklin smiled and sipped at some coffee he had chilled in the icebox.

"How's that?" Kellerman asked.

"Nothing of import, it's just that I don't

normally have many people calling on my residence. I tend to be a solitary person."

"I'm kind of the same way," Kellerman said, taking out a pad and a pen.

"Did you buy that painting?" Ronald asked, pointing to a piece that was framed on the wall.

"No, my young friend, I painted it."

Ronald stared at the painting for a moment, and then at Franklin.

"You're that Franklin Hessler?" He asked in disbelief.

Franklin nodded.

"I'm a big fan of your work, Mister Hessler; I have been since you came to the states."

This seemed to spark something in Kellerman's eyes.

"You did then, immigrate?" Kellerman asked.

"I did not pick up this accent in your Hollywood." Franklin smiled.

"Of course. I just meant that some people enter illegally. You know, forging documents and that sort of thing. But of course, you entered legally."

Franklin nodded. "Of course."

"Of course. Do you mind if I ask where you immigrated from?"

"I left Germany after the war and lived in Spain for some years, but I decided we would be better off in the United States."

"Were you active in the war at all?"

"A simple combat officer on the Eastern Front, nothing more."

"Stalingrad?"

Franklin nodded.

"I see." Kellerman closed the notepad and leaned back in his chair. "Mr. Hessler, a young man was the victim of a hit and run here in your neighborhood. There is evidence to indicate that after the driver hit him, this person then got out of the car and delivered a blow to the victim's head."

"I read of the hit and run in the newspaper, but nothing of the other activities. That is a shame."

"Yes." Kellerman looked around the house. "Well, I won't take up any more of your time, Mr. Hessler. I'm sure you've got some work to do of your own."

"Always."

Franklin showed the two policemen to the

door, wishing them good luck in finding the driver.

"One other thing I should mention," Kellerman said, turning toward Franklin. "The victim was Jewish. They took his star of David."

"It sounds, Inspector, as if you may be dealing with a hate crime of convenience."

"That's just what I was thinking."

A thin fog had settled into the Sunset District as the two Inspectors walked along the cracked concrete sidewalk.

"You're a fan?" Kellerman asked, stopping mid-stride.

"He's a great artist," Ronald responded.

"What does he paint?"

"He used to paint classical scenes from Shakespeare, and I recall Dante's Inferno was one of his favorites. He had a brief impressionist period—"

"Okay, forget I asked," Kellerman cut him off. "What's your impression of him?"

"German immigrant." Ronald shrugged.

"Kind of an odd guy, but not much more to him."

Kellerman pulled out a crumpled pack of cigarettes only to find it empty. "Christ. Something's up with him."

"You think he did it?"

"Nah." Kellerman shook his head quickly. "Guy like that doesn't have a reason to. If he wanted to kill Jews, he'd do it another way, it wouldn't be this passive-aggressive bullshit. He'd be shooting them from rooftops."

"So, what's your problem with the old guy?"

"I'm not buying the line officer bullshit. He's too put together for that. He feels like SS to me. I wonder if Mossad's on him?"

"You want to make the call?"

"To the Nazi Hunters?" Kellerman thought about it for a moment. "No. Not yet. I wouldn't want to toss them a bum lead and make us look like a bunch of asses. Might run him through Interpol though. See what comes up."

Franklin Hessler stood in his living room staring at some framed photos on the mantle, obviously deep in thought. His grandson Will had been painting in the backyard through the entire exchange with the Inspectors, but art had now taken a backseat to the events that were unfolding in the Hessler household.

Franklin saw Will standing in the doorway to the garden and smiled softly.

"You are curious as to what those policemen wanted, am I correct?"

That was only part of it, but Will nodded his affirmation.

"A young man was killed in a hit-and-run accident. He was a Jew, and so I suspect they are questioning anyone that may have had cause to kill a Jew." Franklin paused. "Perhaps though, you are wondering about Isabelle's grandfather, and how the two of us can occupy the same room at the same time without throttling one another into the afterlife?"

Will was unsure what to say, and so he remained silent.

Franklin laughed out loud and waved for Will to sit down at the kitchen table while he prepared lemonade for the two of them.

"Aren't you afraid he'll tell someone who you are? That they'll come to take you away?"

"Like Eichmann?" Franklin asked.

Will nodded.

"I am a small fish, William. I find it unlikely that anyone would spend the time and energy necessary to extract me from this country for past crimes, real or imagined."

CHAPTER 6

"Hessler. Diane Hessler." Kellerman thought on the name for a moment as he and Ronald stood in front of the unassuming house. "Same family, you think?"

Kellerman dropped his cigarette to the ground and stubbed it out with his heel.

"Only one way to find out," Ronald replied.

Ronald reached out with one long finger and rang the doorbell. The two inspectors waited silently for the woman of the house to answer.

"May I help you?" Diane Hessler asked with a sweet smile upon opening the door to find two strangers on her front step. Kellerman and Stein both had their badges clipped to the lapels of their suits, so it was not difficult to discern that they had arrived on police business.

Kellerman felt his hands lightly trembling as he stood transfixed. He said nothing, and picking up on this, Ronald took over.

"Hello Miss Hessler, we're just investigating a hit and run in the neighborhood."

For the next few minutes John Kellerman stood in silence as Ronald conducted the short interview. Diane Hessler seemed very co-operative, but John was unable to break himself out of his trance. Once Ronald finished with the interview he thanked Diane Hessler for her time and walked back down the steps with his partner.

Ronald hadn't seen it. The door had only been open part way. Ronald was standing to the right, and from his vantage point he hadn't seen the goddamned thing. Kellerman had seen it through the sliver of an opening where the hinges joined the door to the frame.

"Hey." Ronald managed to break through by shaking Kellerman's shoulder. With that, the older inspector felt every one of his fifty-five years come crashing down on him, and he slowly sat down on the sidewalk. His hands were shaking again. Not softly, but violently, like the day he ran ashore at Sicily.

"You didn't see it, did you?"

"See what?" Ronald asked.

"When she opened the door... there was a fucking Nazi flag hanging over the fireplace."

"Today some policemen came to grandfather's house," Will said apprehensively as he slowly ate his vegetables at the kitchen table.

"Really?" Diane looked over her shoulder at her son. "They came here as well. A younger man and an older one? The older one with a limp?"

Will nodded.

"Yes, they were asking me about something that happened," Diane said.

"A man was hit," Will said.

"Yes, that is what I was made to understand."

"He was Jewish," Will said quietly.

"I was made to understand that as well."

She set a plate down on the counter, a little

more loudly than she normally would have done and let out a breath.

"Do you not have some homework that needs to be done?"

Will stood and carefully stepped away from the table.

As the darkness of the hallway leading to his room swallowed him, Will heard Diane whisper in German in the kitchen.

"Another Jew burns in hell."

It was late at night, and a bad dream forced Will from his sleep. He walked into the kitchen to pour a glass of water and stood in the glow of the kitchen stove light. His mind was moving at half speed, trying to recall what it was that had haunted his sleep, but to no avail.

Diane Hessler posted all of her bills on the refrigerator so that she could more easily keep track of them. Peeking out from behind the water bill was one for Krendler's Auto Body on Noriega. Will lifted the water bill and read the one beneath it.

Repaired damage to right front fender—paid in full.

. . .

Isabelle's grandparents (Irving and Rachelle Dyer) lived on Forty-Second and Santiago, a reasonable distance from Diane Hessler's home on Forty-Sixth and Ortega, but not too far.

Irving and Rachelle had been married for over twenty years, but they somehow managed to stay perfectly in love. Rachelle worked in a secretarial pool in the Financial District, and Irving worked as a clerk at city hall performing all manner of tasks. Each morning they left the house together and took the Municipal L train from Taraval Avenue into the city and returned the same way in the afternoon.

In addition to the hundreds of books that adorned Irving's shelves, there were also stacks of Hebrew language newspapers in the corners and smaller stacks in odd yet specific places. They were all carefully organized by date, and in the basement, there were large wooden boxes containing thousands of the same newspapers dating back to as early as 1956. Since arriving in America, Irving had friends send him the papers in bulk packages each week. Irving Dyer was a man who felt it was very important to stay connected to the homeland and not forget where he had come from.

"Would you like some iced tea?" Irving asked with a smile, opening the door to the ancient refrigerator.

"Yes, please," Isabelle and Will answered in unison.

As Irving poured the tea, Will stood over one of the Hebrew language papers, attempting to decipher the writings to the best of his ability.

"Are you trying to read?" Isabelle asked.

Will nodded.

"Do you know what it says?" Will asked.

Isabelle scrunched her face up in a feat of concentration.

"Grandfather made me learn, but it's hard to understand sometimes. This paper is much older than the others, nineteen sixty-four," she said, pointing to a column, "It's about the Arabs, and how they formed some type of group to attack the Jews."

"The PLO," Irving's voice said as he handed them the glasses of iced tea. "Yassir Arafat is heading up this group of terrorists. Their goal is the destruction of Israel."

"Who is Arafat?" Will asked.

"An Egyptian who claims to be a Palestinian. Difficult to do as there is no Palestine."

"Why is there no Palestine?" Will asked. "Where did it go?"

"The UN redrew the boundaries after World War Two," Isabelle began. "But the Arabs could not accept a Jewish state side by side with their own, so they attempted to drive the Jews out."

"It did not work out as they intended," Irving finished. "We overcame the Arabs and gained control of the entire region. Now... there is no Palestine."

Will knew that as a non-Jew he had a different perspective on the entire Israel-Palestine affair than Irving and Isabelle. It seemed to him that things were not as cut and dried as Irving made it sound, but then again, having no direct experience with the conflict, he could not be certain.

"It's interesting, this whole other world out there that I know nothing about," Will said, transfixed by the newspaper Isabelle held.

"I could teach you about it, if you wish," Irving said.

"Teach me?"

"Yes. Some history, the language."

"My mother would not approve."

"I understand," Irving said, laying a hand on Will's shoulder and smiling. "And I have no wish to cause tension between you and your family, but you must also decide whether you are going to do things in this life to please them, or yourself?"

"You could teach me Hebrew?"

"Yes," Irving said, "and when I cannot Isabelle would be happy to help you, I am sure."

It was an order to Isabelle from her grandfather, not a request. Irving did not want to push knowledge on Will, but he was very ambitious about spreading his culture.

"You see, William, it is important that Isabelle and her generation know the history of their people. It is very important that all people understand what it was that happened in the camps, and what Hitler did."

"You think that people will forget?" Will asked.

"No. History will remember." Irving looked out the window at the gray clouds rolling across the blue sky. "History will remember."

Will Hessler and Isabelle Dyer began to spend more time together. Will found that he picked up Hebrew very quickly, and absorbed the information he was being taught like a sponge. This was not a great surprise as Will had long ago noted that he did not seem to forget many things, and was already fluent in both Spanish and German.

On a cool San Francisco evening Will stood on the sidewalk in front of his grandfather's house wearing a neatly pressed shirt and tie. The young man had to be presentable for his grandfather's gallery showing. Isabelle had not been invited, due to Will's mother attending.

"I wish you could come," Will said.

"I wish I could too..." Isabelle's voice trailed off, and Will knew what she was thinking. She knew that his mother would never stand for it. "Do you hate her?"

"My mother?" Will asked, confused.

"Yes." Isabelle nodded and bit her lower lip, her brow furrowed in consternation at the prospect of confronting Will's mother again. "I would hate her... if she were mine."

Will was not disturbed by this declaration and felt no ill will toward Isabelle for speaking her mind. He knew that her feelings were correct.

"I cannot hate her. She is my mother. I... don't know what to say."

"I understand, Will. It's not your fault that she is the way she is. At least you turned out okay."

Will smiled and felt a warmth in his stomach.

On occasion, Isabelle would lean in and kiss Will on the cheek by way of saying good-bye, a friendly gesture and nothing more. Once more Isabelle leaned in to kiss him on the cheek, but this time her navigation was skewed by the residence of something new within her heart, and her lips found Will's.

Of Will Hessler's first kiss, he can recall a softness and a stirring in his belly, something on the order of a rebellion of butterflies. It lasted only a moment, and his eyes closed, then opened to find Isabelle bathed in sunlight and reflecting heaven. She smiled, and he couldn't help smiling as well.

"I hope everything goes well at your grandfather's exhibit, Will." Isabelle turned and began walking down the path that would take her home. She looked over her shoulder. "Tell me all about it tomorrow."

The art showing was something of an event for the well dressed and well to do. Men wearing suits, and women in expensive dresses with jewels around their necks. In the center of the room was a large board on an easel with a photo of Franklin Hessler and a short biography below it. He looked very peaceful in the photo, and to read the life he had forged for the biography, you would never suspect anything other than a completely ordinary existence, perhaps even boring.

For the individual that looked closely, who was hungry for the truth of machines and how they work, Franklin Hessler's complete history and everything you would ever need to know about him and his character was contained in the blood and oil on his canvases.

There was a uniqueness, and a sense of menace to Franklin's paintings that was never immediately apparent, and could not be successfully translated unless you knew the truth about the man himself. When asked what a particular painting was about, he would often shake his head and claim to not know. There is a distinct possibility that he truly did not understand what he was painting.

A police officer holding open a large metal door for a small girl dressed in rags. A clerk waiting at a table on a line of people that seems to stretch into infinity. A man digging a giant hole in the frozen snow, surrounded by red autumn leaves.

Translation: An SS man holding open a gas chamber door for a child. A clerk at a concentration camp checking in Jews. A man digging a mass grave surrounded by blood splatters in the snow.

There was a small commotion near the entrance to the gallery and Will turned to see his mother arrive, fashionably late as usual. The attention of all in the room gravitated toward her. She wore a long black dress and a diamond necklace around her slender neck, her gray-streaked black hair swept up into a bun. There was a man with her, one of the people that sometimes came to the meetings at her house late at night, the ones Will tried to avoid. The man was tall with a hard face, and he wore an ill-fitting suit that had obviously not been purchased for him. He looked as if he were the type of man not accustomed to wearing such a suit, and that Diane Hessler most likely had to force him into it.

Will turned away from them, and saw his grandfather, looking every inch the SS commander he had been as he sized up this man that Diane had brought with her. In the rare instance that Diane Hessler chose to let one of her acquaintances meet her father, the results were normally less than satisfactory.

Diane crossed the room, kindly greeting those she knew and introducing herself to those she did not. She instantly became the warm light that all things in the universe gravitate toward. The wearing of this mask was a useful skill for one whose soul was more comparable to a black hole.

The moment that her eyes met her son's they turned cold, only for an instant but long enough to communicate that matters between the two of them had not been reconciled.

Diane Hessler placed her hand on Will's shoulder as she smiled at her father and introduced the stranger she was with.

"Father, this is Greg Sanders. Greg, this is my father Franklin Hessler."

"A pleasure to meet you sir," Greg said, shaking Franklin's hand.

"Yes, I'm certain it is," Franklin responded with a smile. "And your relationship to my daughter is?"

"He is just a friend, father."

"A friend? What kind of friend?"

"I feel as if I am the subject of an interrogation," Greg said, his face not altogether humorless. Even so, Franklin found little humor in the question, and the coldness in Franklin Hessler's eyes was not lost on Greg. Franklin did not like feeling as if young people were being insolent toward him.

"Perhaps that is because you are."

"Why must you behave that way toward any man I bring to meet you? You should feel fortunate that I still deign to bring any logically thinking human within fifty feet of you after everything you have put me through!"

"No one uses the word 'deign' in common speech anymore."

"Do not brush me off that way," Diane snapped.

After Franklin Hessler's declaration as to how he was going to handle Greg, Diane immediately escorted her father to a corner of the gallery and began her own assault.

"What is it you want me to say?" Franklin asked.

"It just seems that if you had your way I would simply obey your every command. Is that what you want? For me to play the obedient daughter, and have no thoughts or opinions of my own?"

"I do want you to make your own choices, but they should indeed be yours. I fear that you are allowing your hatred to choose the direction in which you move."

"What does that mean?"

"It means that you would not be with this Greg if he were not a rabid anti-Semite, like yourself."

"The devil warning me of the perils of evil... besides, what makes you so certain he is an anti-Semite?"

"For one, he is with you." Diane smiled and shook her head as her father spoke. "For two, he is wearing a Nazi Party ring. It is a collector's item now, very popular in the circles of the upper-class anti-Semite."

"And this concerns you because?"

"How many times must I tell you that hating them will profit you nothing? I do not ask you to embrace them, merely to understand why you must learn to tolerate them if you are to function in this society. How many times?" he hissed.

"And how many times do I have to tell you that my hatred for them is the only thing keeping me alive, keeping my heart intact?"

Something about the words stung Franklin Hessler, and looking at his daughter he saw every wrong turn he had taken in her upbringing staring back at him expectantly.

"Perhaps you have too many freedoms, too many comforts," he said.

Diane flinched at this, sensing the

impending threat that had been leveled upon her so many times before.

"Perhaps you do not understand that simply because you refuse to acknowledge the threat that they still pose, does not mean I must imitate your newfound weakness," Diane said, her lips curling back.

"I will not let you destroy yourself as I have watched so many others. I will not allow it. I will cut you off."

"You cannot," Diane said simply.

"And why do you think that is?"

"Because I am your only child, Father." She put a hand on his shoulder and smiled. "I am your Achilles heel." Diane looked away from him and her hand gripped his shoulder harder. "One of us will certainly be the death of the other if we do not come to some agreement."

"You are fortunate to have a mother like Diane."

"Yes," Will said quietly.

Greg had approached Will at the opposite end of the gallery while Will's mother and grandfather were quarreling.

"I've met many people who talk about the problems, about all the things they would do to fix them, but so few are willing to take the actions necessary," Greg said.

"What do you mean?"

Will understood that Greg was one of those men who felt as if he was intellectually superior to others. He had not expected the young man to grasp the nuance of his statement, and when he realized that Will did, Greg attempted to cover it.

"I mean that your mother doesn't mask her opinions, that she doesn't pretend to be someone she is not in order to please others. She is very brave to speak out the way she does."

"Yes. She was very brave when she was chasing my friend off of our lawn."

Greg smiled, somewhat contemptuously.

"Yes, William, she told me about the incident. I'm sure it all seemed very unfair to you at the time, but someday God willing you will understand the depths of the Zionist conspiracy that grips this country before they are able to poison your mind into thinking everything is well in the world."

"You're not like my mother," Will said innocently enough.

Greg's brow furrowed, and he hesitated for a moment before replying.

"How's that?"

"When my mother wants a Jew off of her lawn, she tells the goddamn Jew to get off her lawn. She hangs a Nazi flag in plain sight. After a fashion, I suppose she is brave for acting the way she does even if it is a sick bravery."

"And I am different?"

"Yes. You talk of the 'Zionists.' You don't come right out and say what you feel. You are different from my 'brave' mother. You are a coward."

"I am unhappy."

Franklin Hessler sat in the garden with his hands folded over one knee, studying his grandson intently. Truly, this was not news to him. Ever since the showing at the gallery, and Diane's introduction of Greg, Franklin had sensed an even more pronounced shift in relations between mother and son.

"In what way?" he asked.

"Ways." Will paused, attempting to choose his words carefully. He knew that his grandfather had a bad habit of switching loyalties between daughter and grandson at the most inconvenient of times. "Mother is becoming... darker. These people she meets with are rabid Anti-Semites. I think they are more dangerous than she believes them to be."

"Or perhaps your mother is more dangerous than you think."

This surprised Will. Although he knew that his grandfather privately had reservations about Diane's friends and some of her actions, he had never directly said anything about it. Perhaps Franklin Hessler thought that his grandson was too young to be discussing very serious matters with, and was wary of saying something that might pit son against mother, more than they already were.

"What are you saying?" Will asked.

"William, you are growing up, becoming a man. Soon enough you will be on your own, and you will have to make difficult decisions. It is my unfortunate duty to be the one to tell you that the difficult decisions begin now, at this moment." Franklin paused and rubbed his eyes.

For the first time, Will saw him not as his grandfather, but as the brokenhearted father he had become. "Your mother is unhinged. She has been ever since Argentina, since what happened there. I thought that perhaps in time her heart would heal, but I see now that this was an old man's foolish dream."

Franklin could see the expectant look in his grandson's eyes. Will Hessler knew that something had happened in Argentina before he was born, and that it had changed his mother.

"What happened in Argentina?" Will asked.

Franklin studied his grandson for a moment, but knew that the truth Will was standing at the doorway of could never be revealed.

"I cannot say," Franklin said. "Just know that the world is a terrible place."

Will wanted to push his grandfather, to get to the truth of what had happened, but he knew he should not. Instead he dug for a different truth.

"Did she hit that boy?" Will asked. "The one the policemen were asking about?"

"Yes."

. . .

"I killed him!"

It all came out. Franklin told his grandson how it had happened, how late in the night Diane arrived at his door, banging on the wood frame frantically despite the presence of a doorbell. He had only heard the banging, and it being late at night he crossed the living room silently, with his nine-millimeter Berretta behind his back.

The fog hung low in the streets of the Sunset the night it happened. Diane said that was why she hit him, because she couldn't see the boy crossing the street in front of her. Admittedly she had been driving too fast, but it hadn't been intentional.

"I kicked him."

Diane's hands shook and she balled them into fists. She gritted her teeth, and the animal that Franklin saw before him was not the daughter he knew. This animal had swallowed his little girl whole with its shark's teeth.

"We can do it again," she whispered in a raspy voice. "Not with the war and the chambers, we don't need that here. People are hungry for a change of any kind. They want an enemy that we can provide. An enemy that is in fact already right in front of them!"

"What are you talking about?"

"The Jews!" she snapped. "One here, one there. Sometimes in groups, or guerilla attacks against their beloved social gatherings and temples. It's unrealistic to think we could kill them all, I know that, but we could at least have this country. We could inspire fear in their hearts and drive them from this place! Tonight, after I hit that man, it was the first time I've felt alive since Argentina!"

Franklin Hessler considered himself to be a gentleman. To his knowledge, he had never struck another human being outside of war. He was as surprised as Diane when his hand lashed out and slapped her across the face. For a moment she didn't draw breath, stunned.

"I will not travel this road twice!" Franklin growled. "Not with you, not with anyone. Do not speak of these things to me!"

Diane began to cry, great heaving sobs drawn from the depths of her soul. Franklin pulled his daughter to him and held her close as tears filled his eyes.

"It's going to be okay, Diane. We will get through this. You are my daughter."

After this revelation Will knew that things could never be the same. He went that night to the emptiness of his mother's house. He understood for the first time that it was a house, not a home. Will silently walked past his mother's bedroom and saw her passed out on her bed amid a pile of papers. Passed out, not sleeping. Loss of consciousness after working at something sinister for too long.

In the hallway, the phone rang and Will snatched it off of the hook. He peeked into the room to see that his mother remained asleep.

"Hello?"

"William?" Isabelle's voice carried across the line.

Will was surprised to hear from her. He hadn't expected to hear or see Isabelle until she returned from her summer course.

"Isabelle?"

"Yes, It's me."

"Are you back?"

"No, I'm still at the college. How is everything back there, have you been to see my grandparents?"

"Yes, once every day or so."

"My grandfather isn't pestering you too much, is he?" She laughed.

"No, not too much. I'm still learning a lot."

"How is your speech?" she asked in Hebrew.

"Fine. I am becoming more comfortable thinking like a Jew," Will replied in Hebrew with a private smile.

Everything went black.

"What language is that? What are you saying?" Diane snapped frantically, eyes wild and wide.

Will was stunned, and turning to face the wall he saw a crack in the plaster where his head had struck it. He tried to say something but could only stutter. Diane dragged her grown son to his feet and pushed him against the wall. Her strength was surprising.

"What language is that?" she shouted.

"Hebrew!" Will snapped, tears streaming down his cheeks.

Diane slapped Will hard across the face

and he reacted without meaning to, shoving her away from him and into the wall.

"You are a Jew now, is that it? I knew that letting you play with the Jew girl was the wrong decision!" She balled up her fists and punched the wall, leaving another crack in the plaster.

"There is nothing wrong with learning!"

"You will not speak that language in this house! Tell me, what am I to do with a boy like you?"

"Will you kill me too?"

The words stopped Diane in her tracks. The look of shock on her face was inescapable. For the first time, the playing field had become level.

"What do you think you know?" she asked more slowly, quietly. She was calculating her words, calculating what threat Will Hessler posed. He was no longer her son, but just another chess piece.

"I know everything. You should be more careful with your receipts."

She looked down at the floor. Perhaps with some shame, but more likely with a fear that her son would contact the police.

"I'm not going to say anything." Will paused. "But I will continue with my studies."

Diane looked at her son for a long moment and then straightened herself out.

A tension as taut as any hangman's noose hung in the air between them.

"You will leave my house," Diane said slowly.

"I will do nothing of the sort," Will shot back. "This is my house too."

Diane smiled, and reaching out she placed a hand on her son's shoulder.

"Sleep well, William. Tomorrow is a new day."

It was a threat. Will Hessler knew this, and that evening he packed his things and walked the short distance to this grandfather's house. Franklin Hessler answered the door in his night robe to find his grandson on the front step carrying a suitcase, a bruise across the side of his face where it had struck the wall.

Franklin touched the bruise.

"Your mother?" Franklin asked. It was the only possible answer.

Will nodded.

"You were right," Will said. "She is unhinged, but it's more than that. That man Greg and these people she meets with at night, when she hangs the blankets over the windows. I go for walks when it happens, but I know who they are. I know what they want to do."

"They are an element of the American Palestinian Freedom Co-operative," Franklin said as he led his grandson inside and closed the front door.

"You're familiar with them?"

"After I met Greg—your mother's friend Greg, I began doing some research on the subject. I have a few friends within the police department. Greg was questioned in association with the bombing of a synagogue in New York City."

"Did he do it?" Will asked.

"He definitely was connected to it. I'm not certain if he conducted the actual operation. I have the tendency to believe he is the type of man who orders others into battle and does not take risks himself. For a man like that, finding someone like your mother is like stumbling upon a goldmine. Her rabid anti-Semitic views make her the perfect instrument for his little crusade." Franklin sounded disgusted as he said this. One might think it was because of the viciousness of a man like Greg fighting a war against the Jews, but it was more a matter of respect. In Franklin Hessler's mind, what he had done was honorable because he faced his enemy. Greg attacked and hid like a coward.

"What will you do?"

Franklin looked at his grandson with a certain cold precision in his eyes.

"She has dug herself into this hole, put herself out there to be used by this jackal. I should leave her to the ends she has created for herself." He turned on the kitchen stove to prepare some tea. "But I will not. You, however, need not concern yourself with any of this. For now, we will drink some tea."

CHAPTER 7

I sabelle Dyer returned from her summer college program, and all the things that had been left unspoken between her and Will for so long were finally given a voice.

Isabelle's grandmother Rachelle lost her job in the city, and in place of that began doing more volunteer work at the Synagogue on Twenty Fifth Avenue, Congregation Chevra Thilim. The Dyers were fortunate in that Irving received a promotion and a raise the same month that Rachelle lost her job.

Will did not see his mother for two weeks. During those two weeks he barely thought of her a handful of times. Banishing the memory of his mother from the hallways of his mind was easier than he thought it would be. Perhaps this was because he now understood that she was dangerous, not only to Jews, but possibly to him as well.

Will and Isabelle began taking tours around the city. They had seen it all before, but being together colored the wharf, and the parks, and the rest of the city differently than when it had been their parents or grandparents dragging them around. They kissed time and again, but for some reason never spoke of it, or talked about the possibility that they were in love.

Will continued his studies, both of art and of Judaism. Interrupting these, however, were three days in January. Three days that would change the way Will looked at his grandfather, and everything else.

Franklin Hessler was normally a very outgoing man, quick to smile and joke, easy to talk to. In the entire course of Will Hessler's memory, he could barely account for a day when his grandfather did not talk to him extensively about one thing or another until that Tuesday in January when the old man went silent.

Franklin had a small workshop in his garage, and from that room Will heard the sound of machines running, and occasionally small pops or sounds like air swishing through a tube. Other times his grandfather would be sitting at the kitchen table with maps and a notebook, writing furiously. He worked on some type of dyeing project in the laundry room sink, wearing a hospital mask to protect himself from the fumes given off by the various chemicals he was using. On that Thursday, Will Hessler may as well have not even existed as far as his grandfather was concerned.

By Friday, Franklin began speaking to his grandson again, but not much. He gave only simple instructions on where Will should find his meals, and what time he expected him home. When Will did come home, his grandfather was nowhere to be found.

The next morning, Will awoke to muffled sounds coming from the backyard. Still in the beginning stages of being awake, he walked through the kitchen door and onto the wet lawn, dew seeping between his toes.

Franklin Hessler stood near his herb garden, digging at a slow and deliberate pace. Near his feet and off to the side lay a large object wrapped in garbage bags and secured once again with duct tape. If Will had been fully awake and thinking more clearly, he never would have asked his next question. "What are you doing?"

Franklin was clearly surprised to see his grandson.

"William, I am burying some garbage. Nothing more."

Franklin leaned against his shovel and looked out to the horizon. He turned back to Will.

"If anyone were to ask you, you never saw me burying this garbage. Do you understand?"

Will nodded his understanding.

"Because it is illegal to bury garbage in one's yard, but I must make an exception in this case. Now go and fix yourself some cereal, I will be done in an hour or so."

A disturbance was reported in the blue house on Balboa Street, at the corner of Balboa and

Twentieth Avenue. First, they reported some shouting, then someone screaming No! No! No! Then the sound of a window breaking and several flashes of light, six to be exact. The witness reported seeing someone fall down the front steps of the house and into the street. The man got up on his knees and held his hands in front of his face before crumpling back to the pavement. After that the witness became frightened and closed her curtains.

Inspectors Kellerman and Stein arrived on the scene at about five in the morning, on the tail of the crime forensics team. They entered the primary crime scene whereupon Stein was immediately instructed to place his hands in his pockets to avoid contaminating the scene. The forensics investigator knew he'd probably be read the riot act if he tried to pull that with Kellerman, so he decided against it.

"Okay, here's the grand tour." The F.I. walked them into each bedroom and pointed out where the four victims had been sleeping before they were awoken and rounded up in the living room.

"He took them in the living room?" Ronald asked.

"Right." The F.I. led the two inspectors into the living room. "I marked the impact points in the carpet with tape." The inspectors saw small white X's taped onto the carpet, three of them. "This guy was very clean. He woke them up with a gun in hand and ordered them into the living room. From here he had them lay face down on some kind of drop cloth and started executing them. I'm not sure about the impact points, I just did a little spatial science to figure out about where they would be."

"Spatial science?" Ronald raised an eyebrow.

"I look at the size of the room, this one being pretty small. Calculating the size of the men who lived here and adding a standing male and the angle of escape of the man who died in the street, I can figure about where the heads were when these men were shot. Got it?"

"No, but continue."

"Thanks," the F.I. grunted. "Now, for whatever reason, the fourth male was able to get to his feet and make a break for the door before the killer noticed. I don't quite know why because this guy was very clean—"

"Tunnel vision?" Kellerman asked.

"Maybe." The F.I. nodded. "Anyway, the guy managed to get to the door before the killer noticed and fired on him. First round missed and went wild. Second round tagged the runner in the back, at which point he fell down the steps. I figure the back from the blood spray and angle of descent, maybe a lung penetration. He landed on the sidewalk, got up on his knees to beg for his life, and the killer put him down."

"Wait a minute. Where'd the wild shot go?" Kellerman asked.

The F.I. pointed across the street to a house with a broken window.

"Shitty deal, one in a million. Killer was using a silenced nine-millimeter, not a weapon known for long distance shooting, but the round managed to cross the street, break that window, and nail the old woman that lives there in the neck. She's in the ICU at St. Mary's. She won't make it," the F.I. said matter-of-factly, as if he were reading his grocery list.

"We don't get a lot of assassinations out here in the Richmond," Ronald thought aloud.

"How about domestic terrorism?" The F.I. asked.

"What's that?" Kellerman perked up.

"You'll love this."

In the basement of the house on Balboa and Twentieth, the investigative arm of the San Francisco Police Department had found detonating chord, blasting caps, and traces of explosives. In addition to this, they found photos and blueprints of several local synagogues and Jewish cultural centers.

"Jesus Christ," Ronald whispered.

"Nobody's crying for these assholes tonight, Inspector," the F.I. said, holding up some waxy paper. "See this? This is C-4 wrapping, some serious shit. These guys meant business."

"Now I really want to find this killer," Kellerman mumbled as he pulled out a pack of cigarettes. "So I can buy him a drink."

"You know you can't smoke that in here," the F.I. snapped.

Kellerman scowled and tucked the cigarettes back in his pocket.

"No smoking in the crime scene," he mimicked the admonishment he had heard so many times before.

"So we've got the wrapper," Ronald said

with a slight waver in his voice. "Where are the contents?"

Inspector Stein skipped down the front steps of the house and onto the street. Kellerman walked after him, expecting him to slow down to accommodate the one-legged Inspector's slower gait.

Ronald kept walking down the street.

"Where are you going?" Kellerman asked.

"My sister lives out here. I'm going to call her and tell her to stay out of the synagogues until we crack this thing."

"You're not a very observant Jew, are you?" Kellerman asked.

"No. What does that have to do with anything?"

"Ronald, Tomorrow's Roshashanna. There's no way to keep her out of the synagogues."

Ronald stopped and looked at Kellerman. Kellerman had realized it as soon as he made the statement.

It would happen tomorrow.

. . .

"I want to know what you did!"

Diane Hessler stood in the doorway of her father's house, her face painted with rage.

"I did nothing. What are you talking about?"

Franklin did not invite her in; he only stood in the doorway as immobile as stone.

"The police came to my house today. The same officers who were investigating the death of that boy!"

Franklin stared at her for a moment as if waiting for her to continue and then shrugged.

"So? What is this to me?"

"Greg has been reported missing! Along with three of his friends!"

"Perhaps they went on holiday," Franklin replied calmly.

"Their house was torn up, and there were bullet holes in the wall! Someone murdered them!"

"I grow tired of these riddles. What does this have to do with me?"

"You killed them!" She shouted, sticking a finger in her father's chest.

There was a loud wooden smacking sound as the door hit her, and then Diane Hessler stumbled backward down the front steps. Franklin had kicked the door shut. It was more of a defensive reflex than something deliberate, but he showed no signs of remorse as the door swung back open, having bounced off of his daughter's arm.

"So, you are a Jew lover now too?" She asked, tears in her eyes as she stood on the lawn, holding her arm where the door had closed on it.

"Do not speak to me of love for the Jews!" Franklin snapped. "You know nothing! You may destroy yourself, but I will not stand idly by and allow it to happen!"

"You take my son, now you murder my friends! Is that it?" Diane shouted.

"Lower your voice, girl," Franklin said coldly.

Diane said nothing, only stared at her father.

"It does not matter. What you have done changes nothing. I have already taken the steps necessary to secure our future."

"What have you done?" Franklin asked, afraid of what the answer would be.

"What is right," Diane answered.

. . .

"You think the old man killed them?" Ronald asked, sipping on his soft drink as he and Kellerman watched the drama play out on the Hessler lawn from their unmarked car parked down the street.

"She sure seems to think so," Kellerman replied.

"You going to roust him?"

Kellerman thought on it for a moment and shook his head. "No. You're going to."

"Me?"

"Yeah. He's too comfortable with me. I don't want you hauling his ass in, just give him a good once over, try to get him to slip up."

"You think he'll slip?"

Kellerman looked at Ronald incredulously and laughed. "Ronald, the guy was a Nazi officer. Do I think he'll slip up and fill out a full confession? Not in a million friggin' years. It'll be good practice for you though, and who knows? Maybe he'll at least feel sorry for you and toss you a bone, a hint of some kind."

"You're kidding."

"No. Hessler's just that arrogant. That's

the good thing about him having been a Nazi officer who escaped the wrath of the Allies and pretty much everyone on planet Earth. Guys like that don't tend to be too modest, SS or not."

"What are you going to do?"

"I'm getting a warrant for the daughter's house. She's full of rage, but I'm not thinking a lot of brains. Maybe we'll get lucky and turn something up. If she had something to do with what we found in that house on Balboa, maybe we'll get a lucky break and find a crate full of C-4."

Franklin Hessler answered the door to find the Jewish Inspector of Police that had been at the house before. The young man was holding his badge out for Franklin to see, and that was how Will knew that something serious had happened.

"Franklin Hessler?" Ronald asked.

"Yes, may I help you?" Franklin smiled.

"May I come in?"

Franklin stepped back and waved the Inspector in. Ronald walked into the living room briskly, looking around the house as he did so, seeming to be searching for something.

"Have you seen your daughter today?"

"Yes, I have. She was just here."

"Did she say anything to you?"

"Nothing of consequence. She has had a disagreement with her son, and I am watching after him."

"What sort of disagreement?" Ronald asked.

"If it is all the same Inspector, it is a private matter, and I would prefer that things stay that way."

"Understandable," Ronald replied, walking back into the kitchen. Ronald peered out the window for a moment, and saw the freshly turned earth in the garden. The inspector looked to where Will was sitting in the living room with his sketchbook. "Your grandfather's been doing some gardening, hasn't he?"

"Mostly just burying things," Franklin answered for Will. "Trash for the most part."

"Are you aware it's against the law to bury trash in your yard?"

Franklin nodded and shrugged.

"Nobody is perfect."

.   .   .

Both warrants were served simultaneously. One to dig up Franklin Hessler's yard, and one to search Diane Hessler's house on Ortega Avenue. Ronald had called into Kellerman to get his warrant, and the judge commented that it was the first time he had authorized search warrants for a father and daughter together.

Ronald Stein stood patiently in Franklin Hessler's backyard as the forensics team dug up the older man's garden. All the while Franklin sat in a lawn chair drinking iced tea and making suggestions that he would like it if they would remember where the flowers were so that they could replace them after they finished playing in his garden. The arrogance of the SS-SD officer was peeking out of the old man.

"We've got something," one of the workers said. For a few more minutes they cleared dirt, and then slowly pulled a large canvas bag out of the ground and lay it on the lawn.

"What are you thinking you will find in there? Just curiosity, you understand," Franklin asked.

Ronald gave him a dirty look and turned

back to the canvas bag as the forensics man cut it open. He reached inside and pulled out a handful of garbage.

"I know it is wrong, but they only pick it up once a week, and my garbage can is very small."

Diane Hessler was not nearly as easygoing as her father when Inspector Kellerman came to her house with a search team and served her with the warrant.

"You cannot come into my home!" she shouted at Kellerman as he pushed his way through the door and into the entryway.

"I just did." Kellerman stopped and grabbed her arm. He looked at the bruise where Franklin Hessler had slammed the door on her. "What is this?"

"I fell!" she snapped at him.

"Right."

For an hour the team tore the house apart, searching it from garage to attic and finding nothing.

"We found your boyfriend with a bullet in his head, Diane," Kellerman said, sitting down across from her in the living room as the search team wrapped things up. "Him and a few other unfortunates."

"I don't know what you're talking about," she said curtly.

"Do you know what C-4 is?"

"Some sort of automobile engine?" she smiled slyly.

"Cute. It's an explosive. You're not a big fan of synagogues, are you?"

"I am not a big fan of whore houses either, what is your point?"

"It looked like Greg was interested in blowing up some houses of worship. What do you think about that?"

"I have no thoughts on it." Diane seemed to consider it for a moment. "Why, should I?"

Kellerman eyed her and smiled. "You're so good at playing dumb, I almost think you're not playing." Kellerman stood up and walked around the kitchen. He stopped and looked at a business card for public storage on the refrigerator. Pulling the card off he turned it around and looked at the unit number written on the back. "Almost."

The third warrant Judge Davis issued for Inspectors Kellerman and Stein that day was for a public storage facility on Geary and Masonic, unit number twenty-two.

Diane Hessler sat in the back of the San Francisco Police squad car in handcuffs as the police forensics team went over the storage unit. In the low hanging fog, John Kellerman stood expectantly, watching the unmarked cruiser wind its way through the parking lot toward him. Ronald Stein parked the vehicle and stepped out. By the way he wouldn't look Kellerman in the eyes, John knew the news wouldn't be good.

"Nothing." Ronald shook his head. "We dug up half the old man's yard looking for bodies and didn't find shit. What about you? Dispatch told me you called in for a new warrant."

"Nothing in the house aside from some scary Nazi paraphernalia, but I did find a business card for this place with that unit number on it," Kellerman said, pointing to the unit.

"How long have you been here?"

"Half an hour. Apparently, her boyfriend tossed the lock the office gave them and put his own custom job on it. Took us until about five minutes ago to crack it off with a blowtorch. F.I.'s in there right now giving the unit a once over."

"Inspector!" The shout came from inside the unit, and Kellerman and Stein walked toward it as a forensics team member waved them in.

The F.I. officer from the crime scene on Balboa stood inside the storage unit, pointing to various objects as he talked.

"Half a block of C-4, blasting caps, det chord, cases of nine mil ammunition, more blueprints and photos of synagogues. These weren't photos clipped from a magazine, they were all taken with the same camera."

"This is all kinds of bad," Ronald said, kneeling down and looking at the photos.

The F.I. looked at Kellerman, and the inspector could see something like fear in the man's eyes.

"What?"

The F.I. didn't say anything, he just pointed at a calendar taped to the wall with a day circled in red.

"That's today," The F.I. said quietly.

"Jesus Christ," Ronald whispered, turning to Kellerman. "You were right."

"Get her out of the car, now!" Kellerman yelled. Reaching beneath his coat, he pulled out his pistol and held it behind his back.

"What are doing?" Ronald asked.

"Shut your mouth!" Kellerman snapped, pointing a finger at Stein. "I'm not playing any more games with this woman!"

An officer escorted Diane Hessler into the storage unit, her hands still cuffed.

"Close that door," Kellerman said, and the officer complied.

"You know what's happening today, don't you?" Kellerman asked, grabbing Diane.

"Of course."

"They're blowing up a synagogue," Ronald said.

"Many Jews will die today. Just the beginning of a new Holocaust."

"All right you sick bitch, I'm giving you one chance! Where is it? Tell us how to stop it!"

Diane smiled and looked at Ronald. "Are any of your family in synagogue today?" She then turned to Kellerman. "I like you, inspector, because you're good. You won't do

anything, you are a police officer and police officers are supposed to protect and serve,
correct?"

John Kellerman was in fact a good man.
Despite a reputation as a tough guy, he had
only ever been in a few fights outside of the
war. He took no joy in causing people pain, and
many times that had been a liability in a line of
work where you have to be tough. In spite of his
good nature, somewhere deep inside of him a
switch had been tripped, and he lashed out.

Ronald wanted to react, to do something to
stop Kellerman when the man grabbed Diane
by the throat and slammed her against the wall.
Instead, he was rooted to his spot by the knowledge that there really was no other way, not if
he wanted to see his sister alive again. Even
when Kellerman shoved the barrel of his
revolver into Diane's mouth, breaking her teeth
and eliciting a choked scream, Ronald did
nothing.

Diane collapsed to her knees and struggled
against her handcuffs.

"You tell me where it is! Now!" Kellerman
shouted, cutting off her windpipe with his grip.
"You tell me where that bomb is, or as God is

my witness, you will die in this shed! You tell me!"

Kellerman took the barrel out of her mouth and put it to her forehead. Blood dripped down her face from the muzzle. Diane didn't shake, or cry, or beg. She simply stared at him, secure in the knowledge that she had been right. He was a good man and would not kill her.

Kellerman's eyes teared up and his hand shook.

"There are women and children in those synagogues. You tell me where it is!"

Diane bared her smashed teeth and spat blood, "Grind the children to meat before they can grow up, get the women before they can breed again. Cut off the beast's head and it will die."

Will Hessler was standing in the backyard of his Grandfather's house when it happened. The young man was mulling over all the holes the police had dug, and then not even bothered to fill in. It seemed to him that if you were going to dig up a person's yard based upon the presumption that they had done something bad and then you discovered they had not, you should fill the holes back in.

It didn't sound like explosions you hear in movies; it was more like a dull thump. The ground shook beneath Will's feet and windows rattled in their panes. Franklin came running into the yard.

"Are you okay?" he asked, grabbing Will and checking for any wounds.

"I'm fine. What was that?"

"Into the car, now."

Franklin Hessler showed no outward emotion as he drove through the avenues, toward the sound of the explosion, and the slowly rising smoke plume they soon saw. The sound of sirens rang out in the distance, heading in the same direction.

Will had seen many photographs of World War Two, and most were of different scenes of devastation. The scene they came upon looked like one of the photos he had seen of the carnage of war.

The synagogue was gutted to the point that one could see through it, to the buildings on the next street. The survivors of the blast were stumbling, broken, and bloody as they clutched wounds and burnt flesh. Everyone seemed dazed, unsure of what had happened. Inside of the building several dead bodies (and what looked liked they had once been bodies) were strewn about, like rag dolls thrown down by an angry god.

Will turned to see his grandfather walking purposefully across the street to where a child was laying near the entrance of the building. The boy's head was bloody and he was shaking. Franklin knelt down next to the boy and turned the seizing child onto his side.

Police and fire units arrived soon enough, and paramedics ran to where Franklin was futilely trying to save the boy's life. They pulled him away so that they could take over the effort. Franklin had not noticed what both Will and the paramedics had, which was the piece of skull the boy had left behind on the pavement when Franklin Hessler first rolled him onto his side.

Franklin stood amidst the chaos, a man without a purpose. He looked angry, but not angry in the way one would expect a man in such a circumstance to look. He had the appearance of a parent who knows that they are going to have to chastise a misbehaving child.

Looking away from his grandfather, Will saw medics tending to another body lying in the street, the body of a small girl. It was Isabelle Dyer.

They buried Rachelle Dyer on a Sunday in the Jewish cemetery in Colma, south of San Francisco. Isabelle remained stone-faced for days, giving no outward show of emotion. Irving was the same, but Will suspected that this was more from disbelief than anything else. After all that had happened and all they had gone through together, this was how it would end.

Rachelle Dyer, formerly Rachelle Perlman of Palestine, had died with children in her arms, crushed by a section of falling ceiling. The explosives had been detonated by a crude timer in a sequence deliberately set to bring the building down.

According to witnesses, Rachelle had not been in the synagogue when the first explosions occurred; but instead had been late, walking across the street toward the door. The concussive force from the first explosion had blown one of the doors off and it struck her. She managed to get to her feet and went inside to try to help. That was the last anyone saw of her.

The left side of Isabelle's face and her left arm were badly burned. She would carry scars for the rest of her life.

Diane Hessler was taken into custody by the FBI and following her arraignment was remanded for trial by the United States Government. The trial came and went, and she was convicted of thirteen counts of 1st degree manslaughter. She received thirteen life sentences to run consecutively.

"Your total lack of remorse for what you have done shows me that you are not in fact a human being; you are an animal of some sort. So you will be caged like an animal."

Those were the words spoken by the judge at the sentencing.

"Don't you worry William, we'll get your mother out. It may take years and many appeals, but this conviction will not stand." Diane's lawyer laid his hand on Will's shoulder as he spoke, like some sort of surrogate father. Will said nothing and walked away.

After a few minutes of searching through the courthouse, Franklin found his grandson and led him outside. They sat down together on the courthouse steps, and Franklin handed Will a hot dog and a soda. Will stared at them like some sort of foreign objects. Surely this was not the best his grandfather could do to console him?"

"What can we do now?" Will asked.

Franklin shrugged his shoulders and took a drink of his soda.

"We continue to live, as best we can."

"And her?"

"She will live, William. Her life will not be easy, but she has sealed her own fate. We do her no service by letting what she has done destroy our lives as well."

"After all of this, after what she did," Will said carefully, unsure of the response his planned question would provoke. "Do you still believe the same as you did?"

For a moment Franklin looked at Will not the way one would look at a child but at an adversary. Then his eyes softened.

"I will tell you that seeing the bombing of the synagogue has left me shaken. I have not seen anything like that since the war. Even then I was on the inside of a society that thrived on like-mindedness. It is easier to not just accept, but to perpetuate horrific acts when you are surrounded by others who think as you do. So perhaps I am in the beginning of a re-examination of my beliefs."

"How so?"

"I know I do not hate the Jews, but I know I do not love them either. Until now I have tolerated their existence. Nothing more and nothing less. The more time I spend with Irving, the more I begin to think perhaps I have not been as charitable with those people as I should have been. They are entertaining after all. Perhaps that is worth something in the grand scheme of things?"

"Do you think you might try for me, to be more than charitable? To perhaps even be accepting?"

Franklin looked at his grandson for a moment the way one would look at an idiot child who had just asked if paste came in any other flavors, and then a certain sadness overtook him.

"William, I hope you know that I love you,

and that I could not have asked for more from a grandson than you have given me in my lifetime. You fill my heart with joy."

"Thank you. I'm glad."

"Good," Franklin said, and putting a hand on Will's shoulder, he gazed out from the courthouse to the city. "But you must never ask that of me again."

Isabelle would not answer Will's phone calls, which was no surprise to the young man. His mother had been responsible for the death of her grandmother, and with each passing day Will could feel that there was an irreparable rift between the two of them.

On the occasions that Will Hessler could summon up the courage to call the Dyer house, Irving was always very polite to him, but would tell him that Isabelle had no wish to speak to him. Irving suggested that perhaps in the future that would change, and she just needed time to heal both her body and her heart.

Will and Isabelle had been growing closer each day before the bombing, an almost painfully slow evolution of their love for one another.

Now it was over.

Isabelle Dyer had become as much a ghost as her grandmother, but a ghost with a still beating heart and a shattered compass.

CHAPTER 8

Strangely enough, Diane Hessler's act at the synagogue brought Irving Dyer and Franklin Hessler closer together. More and more often they would play chess in the front yard, or spend long hours talking about all manner of things.

Franklin told Will on several occasions that he worried about Irving, and that after the man's loss of his wife he might have also lost his hope. It may have only been Isabelle that was holding him together.

"It isn't right, for one man to lose so much," Franklin said.

Will Hessler never visited his mother in prison. The last words exchanged between them had not been kind, and he saw no reason to include her in his life. This was to say nothing of the atrocity she had wrought. He did know from his grandfather that she asked about her son during their weekly visits. Franklin tried to tell Will things about her, things she had said or done, but the young man always tuned him out because he didn't want to hear it. Regardless of how Diane was supposedly changing, she had cost Will the one thing he loved in life.

In the spring of 1975, Isabelle was rushed to St. Mary's Hospital after overdosing on painkillers. Even by that point she had not properly healed, and she could not bear the pain she was living in. Isabelle had taken too many of the pills and nearly died. Will wanted to go to her, to talk to her, and to be there for her, but he could not. He was barred from the hospital at her request. No, not her request. Will Hessler was denied entrance at her demand. During those years, she only ever screamed his name in anger and at the height of her pain. In those days, his name coming from her lips always sounded like an accusation.

· · ·

Franklin Hessler continued the way he always had. It almost seemed as if everything that happened had not sent so much as a ripple through his carefully arranged world, and Will wanted to know why. He needed to know what quality his grandfather possessed that he did not that allowed the old man to ride out the storm without it destroying him.

Will continued to live with his grandfather, but it was almost as if they were living in the same house but in separate realities. Their normal, easy way of talking had changed. Perhaps Franklin feared that Will may begin to change and become like his mother, and perhaps Will feared that whatever his grandfather had done to change Diane Hessler would also take ahold of him like a disease seeping silently into his bones and his soul.

Will had always been comfortable in high school, seeing nothing but a future full of promise. Once his senior year began it felt more like he was living in his own dystopian future. Everyone knew who he was, and more importantly they knew what his mother had done. No one blamed him, and Will knew this, but the reality was so much worse than that. They felt sorry for him.

Will saw Isabelle at school, but never made an attempt to talk to her because he knew what the outcome would be. He watched her walk through the hallways, a small portion of her face scarred from the fire. She wore long sleeves even on hot days, to hide her scarred left arm. Isabelle had never been overweight, but she hadn't been skinny either. She was comfortably someplace in between. Now Isabelle seemed skin and bones, her face gaunt and pale. The Star of David so prominently displayed around her neck since they first met was gone. She had new friends. People he did not know, but knew enough of to be concerned for her.

Then one day she was gone, and the next day and the next day. Finally, after weeks of Isabelle's absence and no answer when he tried to call, Will summoned up the courage to knock on Irving Dyer's door.

"She is gone," Irving said quietly.

"Gone? Where?"

"She has left home, William. She calls from time to time. She is still in San Francisco, but I'm never sure where."

"I don't understand. Why did she leave?"

Irving looked pained, as if he wanted to explain something but was having difficulty with it.

"Isabelle has become addicted to drugs, William. They have a hold over her that is stronger than my own."

This devastated Will. He thought he knew Isabelle. He thought he knew what kind of person she was and what her desires and fears were. Had she really changed so much? Had his mother's act of terror broken her to such a degree?

The pain from Isabelle's burns had not vanished once the wounds scarred over. She became addicted to prescription painkillers. After she had overdosed and been taken to the hospital to have her stomach pumped, the doctors cut back her medications to almost nothing out of fear that she would kill herself. In the absence of proper medication, Isabelle began self-medicating. She started with marijuana and escalated from there. Irving tried everything he knew to help her but was inexperienced in such matters, and unsure of how to react to what he was seeing.

Irving watched Isabelle begin to tune him out. She spoke to him less and less as the days passed, and when he became intrusive, she completely ignored him. Isabelle put a lock on her door and came and went from the house quickly. She began visibly losing weight and color to her skin. One morning, Irving found her passed out on the lawn. After he revived her and tried to take her to the hospital, Isabelle fought him off and ran away. He broke down the door to her room and discovered just how deep she had descended. He found rolls of twenty-dollar bills, small amounts of marijuana, heroin, cocaine, and assorted paraphernalia.

Irving called the police and put in a missing person's report on her but was told that the resources simply did not exist for the police to track down every child that ran away from home.

That had been two weeks ago.

Will did not know what to say, and so he gave what few apologies he could as well as the offer to help if Irving needed it, though in truth he did not know what he would be able to do. Will Hessler left the house on Ortega street and walked home beneath the morning fog, with the acute sense that this chapter in his life had closed.

Susanne Bonafide was new to the school and new to California. She was a transplant from North Carolina, and while she had heard about the bombing of the synagogue the winter prior, she did not know the details. Specifically, she did not know Will Hessler's name.

In his ongoing state of isolation, Will had begun taking his lunch privately, beneath a large tree outside of the school where he would sit and read the most recent copy he could find of the Jerusalem Post in order to keep up with his Hebrew language skills.

"You can read that?"

Will looked up to find Susanne standing over him.

"Yes."

Will wanted to say something clever to make her laugh, but his mind only scrambled at it for a moment before collapsing into simplicity.

"That's Jewish, right?"

"It is Hebrew, yes."

Her nose scrunched up a little as she pondered what the difference was.

"You don't look Jewish," she finally said, her light North Carolina/Texas accent making itself known for the first time. Will could tell that she made quite an effort to hold it back.

"I'm not. My family is German. A friend of mine taught me Hebrew. She taught me a lot of things about Jewish culture."

"I had a friend who tried to teach me French once, but it didn't quite take."

Will laughed a little and folded up the paper.

"Are you laughing at me?" she asked, but not in a hurt or offended way.

"No. Maybe."

Susanne's family had lived in North Carolina for eight years, beginning when her father was stationed at Camp Lejeune outside of Jacksonville in 1967. Susanne's father, Carl Bonafide, had been a Major who was sent to Vietnam in '68, just in time for the Tet Offensive. Two years later, his left leg was blown off by a landmine and he was sent home. After a year of rehabilitation and a year of light duty he had finally been reassigned to the Presidio in San Francisco and given a job in administration. For a lifelong Infantryman and Force Recon Marine it was a tolerable hell, a sacrifice he was willing to make in order to finish out his thirty years and retire.

Will and Susanne began to date, and soon he found himself becoming more a part of the Bonafide family than his own. Will rarely spoke to his grandfather and knew that as soon as he finished high school the Hessler family would be nothing more than a bad memory. No longer could he rationalize forgiving his grandfather for the things the man had done, and he felt increasingly guilty about allowing Irving Dyer to form a friendship with a villain who had murdered hundreds, perhaps thousands of his people.

Will also knew that if he were to reveal to Irving Dyer the true nature of his newfound friend Franklin Hessler, the man may lose the last buoy available to him in the sea of horrors his life had become.

. . .

Will and Susanne spent their first three months together joined at the hip. It had only taken a couple of weeks for them to fall completely in love with one another. Susanne had been in relationships before, but it was all completely foreign to Will aside from the short time he'd had with Isabelle, a love that the two never even admitted to. This felt different from that, but Will easily identified it for what it was all the same.

Despite what Will had told her about his family, and his incredible reluctance to agree to her request, Susanne insisted on meeting Will's grandfather.

He took her to the house one day after school with the full intention of ushering her in and out as fast as humanly possible. Will found his grandfather working in the garden beneath the sun. The old man wore an absurd gardening hat that he claimed gave him magical gardening powers. Of course, Will had been told this when he was a very young child.

The short time since Diane Hessler's imprisonment had taken its toll on Franklin. No amount of sun could wash the grey from his skin, and the weathered flesh seemed to stretch more tightly across his bones than it once had.

Seeing Will and Susanne enter the backyard, he smiled and straightened up to his full height as they walked across the grass.

"You must be Susanne!" he exclaimed, reaching out a hand to shake hers.

Will noticed a visible hesitance in Susanne's movement as she reached out to shake Franklin Hessler's hand.

"I have heard a great deal about you from William," Franklin said.

This was a lie, albeit a well-intentioned one. Susanne knew that Will rarely spoke to his Grandfather.

"He told me about you as well, Mister Hessler."

Franklin gave Will the briefest of sideways looks as if he were momentarily fearful that in the heat of love his grandson had indeed told her everything. In that split second, Will knew power.

"All good I hope," Franklin said with a smile.

. . .

"He's empty inside, Will. You do understand that, don't you?" Will was unsure how to respond to this as they sat in her father's study. "I'm not trying to hurt you, Will, but it's important to me that you understand that. I have to know that you realize he hasn't changed all that much. I have to know that he hasn't changed you."

"He hasn't. I mean he has." Will shook his head. "I know what you're saying and I know... what he is."

"Can you leave him behind?"

"He's an old man, Susanne. He's all I've got, the only link to my family."

"I know, William. I know it's hard."

"You don't know! You don't know what it's like! I don't have anyone, I don't have anything! I don't even know who my father was. Everything and everyone I ever love turns against me, except for him. I know what he is, I know what he did, but I can't pretend he isn't my grandfather."

Will felt guilty, and again he felt a realization swimming beneath the surface of his flesh that pretending as if his grandfather was a decent man made him complicit in everything Franklin Hessler had done.

"You have to separate yourself from your family, William."

Will stared at her blankly. He could tell from the expression on Susanne's face that she had spent a lot of time thinking this over and trying to find the best way to present it.

After the meeting with his grandfather Will told Susanne everything that was left to know about the former Nazi officer. It was a risk to be sure, but by that point Will felt she would keep his secrets. Susanne may not have agreed with Will's safeguarding of his grandfather's true identity, but he knew she would respect his decision, even if she did not understand it.

"What do you mean?" Will stopped and stuttered a little, "I-I mean, I know what you mean."

"William, they'll destroy you. Eventually they will."

"I can't."

"You have to."

"What would I do, where would I go?"

"Will..." Susanne looked around as if for an

answer. "You are talented. I've seen your paintings, I've read your words, but you've grown up in this bubble with your family. It seems as if you're sitting around waiting for something to happen for you, for something to come your way. For them to change."

"What does that mean?" Will wasn't sure why, but he felt offended, as if she were attacking him.

"I'm not trying to make you feel badly Will, it's just that I think you're intimidated by the prospect of leaving your family and going out into the world. It's not that hard. You get a job, you save up some money, and you find a place to live. I hear people talk all the time about how they can't move on with their lives because of this or that, but most of the time it's just because they're scared."

"Do you really think it's that bad though? That I have to leave right away? I mean, six more months and I can maybe do it."

"You might not have six months, Will." Susanne shook her head and leaned back. "I feel awful, I really do. I'm not trying to be dramatic about this."

Will reached out and took her hand.

"I know."

"You told me, Will, about how he killed those men, about the things your mother did, and I think I probably still don't know all of it. You've been with them for so long that you don't understand what a dangerous situation it is. I'll help you any way I can. We're together, you and I."

"I'm scared. I hadn't even thought of this before."

"Think of it now, Will." Her fingers ran across his hand, tracing his veins beneath the flesh. "Think of us."

"Where will you go, what will you do?"

"I'm not sure. I was offered a job at the kosher deli downtown. I'm friends with the owner. Irving introduced us."

Franklin Hessler stared blankly for a moment as if he were certain he had not heard his grandson correctly.

"A Jew?"

Will stopped his packing and looked up at him.

"Yes, Grandfather, a Jew. I will be working

with and maybe living with Jews." Will threw some more shirts into his duffel. "Ravi said if I couldn't find a place to stay I could sleep in the storage room until I found something." Will thought about this and stopped. "And why is it so strange for me to be friends with a Jew? You are friends with Irving."

"That is different, he- I- I do not understand this." Franklin's face looked confused, and his accent thickened as he became more distressed. "What did I do? What is it I did that is causing this flight?"

"You didn't do anything, Grandfather. You are who you are, and I can't change that." Will stopped what he was saying and sat down on the edge of his bed. "Everything that you believe to be true is not what I believe. Over time I've been accepting things I don't truly believe and remaining silent when I should have spoken."

"Are you saying what I think you are?"

There was a distinct coldness in Will Hessler's eyes as they met his grandfather's.

"If you were not my Grandfather, if I did not love you, I would turn you over to the Mossad tomorrow. That is who I am."

"You would do these things? You would turn your own blood over to a bunch of goddamn Jews?" Franklin's lips tightened, and the color drained from them.

"I told you I won't do it, but I can't live like this. You are wrong in the things you feel, in your ideas about the world. It doesn't even make any sense. What about Irving? He is your friend, right? He's a Jew though, how is that even possible?"

Franklin Hessler's shoulders fell and he stepped back from his grandson in the small room, putting his back to the wall.

"When your mother was first becoming a young woman in Argentina, perhaps twenty or so, I had asked her why she did not have more friends, why she did not care to spend time with the other women in the neighborhood. The few friends she had were acquaintances from the International School, Europeans. I asked her, why not make friends with these Argentinian girls, they seem friendly enough? Do you know what she said to me? You mother said, I do not make friends of animals." Franklin turned to walk out the door. "Perhaps I do."

. . .

The rest of Will Hessler's senior year of high school passed without incident. He worked at the deli on Market Street while living in a boarding house on Gough, and in what little free time he had attempted to keep up with his painting. The only things he ever seemed to produce amounted to nightmares on canvas, pulled directly from the darkness of his sleepless nights.

Susanne decided to pursue a career in medicine and began working on her pre-med courses. This meant that she did not have much time for anything else, to include her relationship with Will. The two continued on as best they knew how, but the strain on their commitment to one another was clear.

Without Susanne's daily influence to keep Will Hessler anchored to the rational world, he began to give in more and more to his artistic side. He smoked and painted furiously into the night, casually tossing aside frivolities such as bathing or cleaning his apartment. This went on for months until Susanne appeared at his door one day to find the young man standing in a room full of urine-filled bottles, some with cigarette butts floating in them. Trips to the bathroom were a luxury that Will Hessler could not afford.

Susanne stood in silence surveying a canvas, this one showing a young man being pulled into the depths of the ocean by a cabal of devils.

"Your family," Susanne said quietly.

Will watched her for a moment.

"I guess. I hadn't thought about it."

Susanne surveyed the apartment again and shook her head.

"I can't do this, Will."

"Do what?" he asked.

"You're living like an animal!"

"This is what you wanted! You wanted me to find myself! Well, here I am!" Will snapped.

"Will, if you keep this up you're going to go crazy like —" Susanne stopped suddenly, a look of horror on her face.

"Like my mother," Will finished the sentence for her.

"Will, I am so sorry. That wasn't my place to say."

"That doesn't mean it's not true," Will said and let out a long breath.

"It's just that when you're like this, you're not *you*."

"So, where does that leave us?"

"Meet me in the middle, Will.

Susanne Bonafide wanted Will Hessler to change, to become more like her idea of what he should be. Since Will had no clear direction of his own, he decided to go in hers.

Will took a job at an upscale gallery in the Financial District explaining to the requisite upscale patrons why Dali and Chagall were everything they needed in life. He wore a suit and tie to work and combed his hair on a more regular basis. He even acquiesced to daily cleanings. He dined weekly with the Bonafide family and allowed Susanne to parade him before her medical school friends. He assimilated. He bent toward the norm, and he felt that this was okay. He still painted in small blocks of confined insanity, but nothing came of it. Will Hessler heard the voice whispering in his ear to let go and that he could never succeed like this. Instead of obeying it Will gagged it with a rag soaked in turpentine and listened to it slowly die.

Susanne became Will's de facto agent, and to his surprise she managed to get him into a showing at a gallery in the Mission. Will wasn't sure how he felt about that. He was glad to have his paintings seen by someone, but he also knew that this work did not encompass his potential in any way shape or form. He felt like a fake. The other fakes just couldn't tell.

CHAPTER 9

Will Hessler woke on a Sunday to an insistent knocking on the door of his Gough Street apartment. Will looked at the clock on the milk crate that passed for his bedside stand and saw that it was nearly ten in the morning.

Sitting up, he rubbed the sleep from his eyes, only to be assaulted again by the rapping on his door.

"I'm coming."

Standing up, Will lit a cigarette and walked across the room, finally opening the door to find Inspector John Kellerman standing in the hallway holding two cups of coffee. Reaching out he handed Will one of the cups.

"It's early, here's some coffee," John said,

handing Will one of the cups as he walked in the door.

Will took the cup of coffee and stared blankly as John walked into the apartment.

"Come on in," Will said after the fact.

"Thanks."

Will closed the door and sat down on a chair. He wasn't quite sure how to regard the man who court records showed had shoved a pistol into his mother's mouth so hard that it broke three of her teeth. Inspector Kellerman had been put on administrative leave and undergone extensive psychological counseling over the incident. In the end all parties involved decided that it had been a fairly appropriate reaction considering the circumstances.

"How did you find me? I just moved here," Will said as he sipped his coffee.

"It's my job to find things, Will. It wasn't hard." Kellerman looked around the apartment. "Your family doesn't know where you are though. I know because I dropped in on your grandfather yesterday. He doesn't understand why you walked out on him."

"Do you?"

"Of course I do. I'm not an idiot, Will. I don't have a shred of evidence to prove it, but I know your Grandfather was no line officer during the war."

"Why don't you follow up on it?"

Kellerman looked surprised that Will would suggest this.

"I'm not partial to the Mossad showing up in the dead of night, throwing a black bag over his head and shipping him out of the country based on my assumptions. Even if he might deserve it. That's not what this country is about. If I can prove it that's something else. Then we take action."

"Are you trying to prove it?" Will paused for a moment and looked hard at Kellerman. "Wait a minute, is that why you're here? You want something from me, to help you get my grandfather?"

"That's not the only reason I'm here." Kellerman drank the rest of his coffee and sat the cup down on the table. "I fucked up, Will. I made a mistake when we took your mom down."

"The gun in the mouth thing, I know. I thought it wasn't a big deal?"

Kellerman looked pained, and Will could see that something was chewing on him.

"The judge who overturned your Mom's conviction last week thinks it was."

For a moment Will went numb and then was surged back to life by a cold shot of fear down his spine.

"What are you saying? They're letting her out?"

"She's set to be released on Friday, after going through an exit program to help her readjust to society."

"Readjust? She wasn't adjusted in the first place! She was responsible for bombing that Synagogue! Oh my God I testified against her!"

"She's not angry with you, Will. Your mom has . . . changed. At least it seems that way."

"You don't seriously believe that, do you?" Will asked.

Kellerman shrugged.

"I'm not sure what to believe. As an outsider looking in . . . she seems different."

"With all due respect, Inspector, you don't really know her, what she's like or what she's capable of."

"I heard the testimony, Will. I know what your mother put you through—"

"You don't even know the half of what happened in that house!" Will felt like there was no getting through to Kellerman, and his mind was racing trying to think of a way to drive his point across. "She was a candidate for the Nazi youth for Christ's sake! She's not going to change."

Inspector Kellerman stood up slowly, seeming to think for a moment about what he should say.

"You'd be surprised how people can change, Will. I'm not saying I believe this horse shit the ACLU lawyer was feeding the judge about how much your mother has changed, but I do think that whether she succeeds or fails might have a lot to do with you."

"You think that, do you?"

Kellerman shrugged.

"Maybe. It isn't easy having parents. It's all wine and roses until they start getting old and you have to take care of them. I know you've had a lot of that. In the end, my mother started losing her mind. It would have been a lot easier for me to just put her in a home, but I didn't."

Kellerman walked to the door. "Maybe just something to think about."

He walked out into the hallway.

"Was it the right thing? For you to take care of her? Would it have mattered if you hadn't? I mean really, do you think it would have?" Will asked.

"I'm not so sure it would have made a difference to her, but I sleep better at night, and maybe I won't have as much to answer for in the afterlife."

"You're missing one thing, Inspector."

Kellerman looked at Will blankly.

"You're assuming I want her to succeed."

"You're not actually considering helping her, are you?" Susanne asked, shock on her face.

Will knew he shouldn't have told her there, where she could make a scene. They were standing in the middle of a crowded art gallery when she snapped at him.

"I'm not saying I'm going to help her, I just don't think I can completely turn my back on her if she asks for my help, even if I might want to."

"The only person you have to help right now is yourself." Susanne looked around and lowered her voice. "You have to remember you're only eighteen. It's not your job to save everyone."

"But it's a different story when you want me to change for you, right?"

"Don't you dare compare me to her, William! I've done everything for you, everything to help you! She hasn't done a goddamn thing for you!"

He knew she was right. Will didn't like it when Susanne started talking to him like a little kid, but she was right. He owed her everything, and he didn't owe his mother a single thing.

Susanne walked out in disgust, leaving Will wandering the gallery alone. He didn't want to stay there, but he was committed to the showing.

Will stood in silence staring at one of his pieces hanging on the wall, a shallow light over it illuminating every swirl, rise and recession of the oils on canvas.

Behind him near the door was some sort of commotion, people gathering around and talking about something. Will had no desire to mix with a crowd at that moment and so he ignored whatever the event was.

People seemed to be interested in Will's paintings and they stood facing the wall the work was affixed to making flattering comments about the pieces. He heard a couple of people claim that they were overly influenced by Dali, but Will already knew that. He had made a real effort over the past few months to not study any other artists, to not go to showings in order to cleanse his pallet. It hadn't done any good. The hole in his work that he couldn't seem to fill from his heart was instead being filled by Salvador Dali.

"It's awfully derivative of Salvador Dali, don't you think?"

"Yes, thank you, I know." Will patted his shirt looking for his pack of cigarettes, which had mysteriously disappeared. Susanne had a habit of removing them while they were embracing and throwing them away. More often than not Will did not even notice. It wasn't the nicotine he was addicted to, but the ritual. The lighting of the cigarette was one of the few things within his control.

"Something's just, I don't know . . . missing?" Franklin said.

"What are you doing here?"

"It's an art showing, I am an artist. It seemed a natural fit," Will's grandfather replied casually.

"I wondered what everyone was making such a big deal about by the front door."

"Now you know."

"The great artist has arrived." Will nodded.

"You say that as if it's a bad thing."

"I guess it all depends on whose shadow you're growing up in."

Franklin Hessler smiled and returned to studying his grandson's painting for a moment.

"I know what this is about," he said.

"Do you now?" Will asked impatiently.

Will looked at the painting of a woman standing up on tiptoes to pick an apple from a tree, not knowing a devil is hiding in the branches. The woman held a butcher knife behind her back.

"You are the apple. Your mother and myself are cast in our appropriate roles."

"What is it you want? You must have come here for a reason other than to appreciate the art," Will snapped, and then immediately felt poorly for it.

"Perhaps that is part of the reason I came. I do not understand where this newfound disdain you show for me has come from. I have done everything within my power to make your life comfortable. When I understood your mother to be wrong, I sided with you against her. When she went to prison, I took you in and would have allowed you to stay as long as you liked. It was you who chose to leave."

"I had to leave. You don't understand. It's not you." Will twitched a little and recanted. "Well, it is you."

"I do not understand."

"Do you not understand that you led Nazi death squads and what that means?" Will hissed.

Franklin shrugged.

"You have known this."

"But I never understood. I never really understood what it meant."

"Dyer," Franklin said and shook his head. "I should never have let you spend so much time with him."

"It's not just Irving. I would have gotten to

where I am, eventually." Will put his hand on his grandfather's shoulder. "This isn't forever. I just feel right now that I have to be on my own."

Franklin nodded, and Will could see that he understood.

"She is being released, you know this?" he asked, turning away from the painting and to Will.

Will nodded.

"Inspector Kellerman came and saw me. He told me about it."

"He came and spoke to me as well. I was surprised to say the least. It is an indication of one of the greatest failings of this country that someone like your mother is being allowed to walk free."

"They say she's changed. He said she's changed, or at least he thinks- maybe- I don't know."

"No one does," Franklin said quietly. "No can know for certain. Not I, not you, none of the psychologists. Only your mother."

"How is Irving?" Will asked. "Has he heard anything from Isabelle?"

Franklin shrugged his shoulders.

"I have not heard from Irving this week, I don't know why. I am sure everything is fine."

Will returned to his empty apartment that night unsure of just what it was that he was supposed to do, and where he now stood with Susanne. That last argument had felt very final, for lack of a better word. Part of him wanted to help his mother, but a larger (and probably more sensible) part was scared to death at the prospect of letting her back into his life.

The day had taken its toll, and Will could feel his bones aching, an ache far too deep for a man his age. He lay down on the bed and had almost drifted off to sleep when the phone rang.

"Hello?"

"Will, this is John, John Kellerman. I need you to come down to Saint Mary's Hospital. It's important." He seemed to hesitate for a moment. "I've got something I think you should look at."

Will caught the late bus down Haight and then

ran up Stanyan to Saint Mary's Hospital. The place was quiet at night and passing the nuns in the hallways gave an eerie feel to it.

He found Inspector Kellerman on the third floor, standing next to the admitting desk. Kellerman looked as tired as Will felt.

"I handled the missing persons case when Irving first filed it, as a special consideration to him considering all that had happened. I'm the contact in case she turned up," Kellerman explained.

A shot of fear raced down Will's spine.

"What do you mean *turned up*?"

"Don't worry, she's still alive. She's okay," Kellerman said, raising a hand in a placating gesture. "She's just had a tough time of it. She overdosed on heroin, Will. It was bad but she'll live. Whoever she was with dumped her in the emergency room and took off. From looking at her I'd guess she's been homeless for a while."

"Can I see her?"

Kellerman looked at the ground and rubbed his forehead.

"Will, there's some other stuff. She... she's five foot six and ninety pounds."

"Jesus Christ. How is she still alive?"

"The human will to live is stronger than you might think. She... shit. She was pregnant, Will, and she lost the baby."

Will was stunned. The entire world ceased to exist for him except for the reality of what his mother's actions had done to Isabelle. Diane Hessler was dead to him.

Isabelle sunk into the white hospital sheets like a homeless spirit, attempting but not quite able to escape the confines of this life. The feelings Will had harbored for Isabelle since last seeing her had not dissipated. Her re-emergence as this wounded animal swallowed whole what was left of his desperate heart.

Maybe what had been between them was not as dead as he once thought it was. Perhaps this could be a second chance to breathe new life into the ghost of what they once were?

Will slept in the waiting room downstairs and ate over on Haight Street, but other than that he didn't leave much. He called in sick to work and waited patiently hour by hour for news of Isabelle's recovery.

On the next day Isabelle woke from her

slumber. The nun told Will that she was conscious, but he did not go in right away. He stood in the hallway for a good five minutes. The man had built up this idea in his head that for whatever reason Isabelle would be happy to see him, that everything would be forgiven and they would melt into each other's arms. He feared that the reality would be quite different.

Will walked cautiously into the room, still unsure of what her reaction would be upon seeing him. Slowly her eyes moved toward him and she smiled.

"She wants me to take her home," Will said to Kellerman as the two stood in the hospital hallway.

Will and Isabelle had been talking about everything from what had happened to people they went to school with, to Will's painting (or lack thereof), to his mother being released from prison.

Isabelle was understandably distressed upon learning that the woman who had been responsible for her burns and the death of her grandmother was being allowed to roam free, but at that point she was too beaten by life to properly articulate the way she felt.

Despite Isabelle's efforts to put on a brave face, Will could see that something was not right with her. She was cold but sweating, looked nauseous and was clearly in pain.

"Home? To her Grandfather's house?"

Will nodded.

"You don't know," Kellerman said in more of a statement than a question.

"Know what?" Will asked.

"Irving Dyer's been missing for over a week now. Why do you think I called you and not him?"

"What happened? Where is he?"

Kellerman shrugged.

"I don't know. I handled the report because I was the officer associated with Isabelle's case. Missing persons division figured I might know something about it, be able to fill in some gaps."

"Who reported him missing?"

Kellerman looked at Will evenly.

"Your Grandfather."

Will had just spoken to his grandfather at the

gallery the night before, and the old man had not mentioned a thing about Irving going missing. Will had asked Franklin specifically about Irving, and still he had not mentioned this. For whatever reason, Franklin had lied right to his grandson's face.

Isabelle was suffering from malnourishment as well as the side effects of the heroin leaving her system. This required that she be transferred to a county facility for several days while she went through this torturous process. Once the worst was over she was released to Will Hessler's custody.

On the taxi ride back to his apartment Isabelle said nothing, only stared out the window at the raindrops cascading down its surface. She was deathly pale. She had taken the news of her grandfather's disappearance in stride. Perhaps it was just too much for her to process.

Will gave her his bed and slept on the floor. He cooked her meals and fed her, held a bucket for her while she vomited and even stood by while she bathed. Anything could happen in her weakened state, and she didn't want to be left alone. Will tried not to look at her body, but there were track marks on her arms from the needles and she was battered and bruised from the abuse of living on the streets. She scrubbed endlessly at her fingernails trying to make them come clean, to no avail.

In the middle of scrubbing, sitting in the tub bent over, Isabelle stopped. Will saw that she was staring at her belly. She ran a soapy hand over it and there was a hitch in her breath.

"Was it a boy or a girl?" she asked quietly, her voice almost inaudible.

"It was too early," Will said quietly. "I don't think they knew."

Will saw the tears flow as they hit her skinny legs, and she shook and cried in the bath, the soap falling from her hands as she clutched her empty belly.

"Oh my God," she whimpered. "What did I do?"

Will knelt down on the floor, his knees hitting the tub in a rush to be near her and comfort her.

"It's not your fault, Isabelle! Don't cry."

"It's not my fault?" she asked incredulously. "It's only my fault! I'm a monster! I've lost everything!"

"Not everything, Isabelle! I'm still here. Nothing has changed between us."

"I ran away! I pushed you away! Don't you understand that? Do you know what I was thinking; the things I wished would happen to you and your family? I've murdered you in my mind a thousand times over! How can you still care for me?"

"I still love you Isabelle," Will said, pulling her into the fold of his arms.

"No!" she screamed, trying to push him away, beating at his chest with her fists. "Don't love me, Will! You can't love me, not after this! I've done things, Will—bad things! You can't imagine what I've done! You can't guess at the things I've done!"

Will held onto her like a vice, like he was desperately trying to hold onto everything in his youth that he had lost to the ravages of a hungry and reckless world.

"It doesn't matter. Nothing matters. We're the only two people in the world. There is no one else. There is no past, no one outside the door. There's nothing, just us."

"You're the only thing I have left, Will," she

sobbed, lying against him. "You and Grandfather."

"What did you do?"

This was the first time Franklin Hessler had to contend with the man his grandson had become, the first time Will was truly angry with him. Will did not have any concrete proof that Franklin had done Irving Dyer any harm, but his instincts said differently.

Several days had passed since the scene at the gallery, and it was about more than just Franklin's obvious lie that he did not know anything about Irving. Susanne was clearly very upset, and she had made no attempt to contact Will. Perhaps that was for the best, as the evolving animal of Will Hessler and Isabelle Dyer was about to shed its skin and become something new.

As for what remained of the Hessler family, Will was at the end of his rope with them both. As far as Will was concerned the Devil or the Mossad could take his grandfather, and he did not particularly care which.

"What are you talking about?" Franklin asked, standing in his doorway.

"Where is Irving? What did you do?"

"I am still at a loss as to what you are talking about."

"I spoke with John Kellerman and he told me you reported Irving missing."

Franklin was obviously surprised by this. He looked away and then back to Will.

"And if I did? What concern is it of yours?"

"He found you out, didn't he?"

"Are you accusing me of something?" He stopped short. "What? What is it you are saying?"

"I don't know what to do here," Will said in exasperation.

"You think I killed Irving."

"Look, you're not making this easy on me."

"Out with it boy!" Franklin thundered. "You think me a murderer?"

"You *are* a murderer!" Will shouted. "A thousand times over!"

A deadly silence descended between the two of them. The old man was shocked by what Will had said, but his face betrayed none of it.

Franklin Hessler was well practiced at keeping his emotions from giving him away.

It wasn't until Franklin let out a breath that Will knew the man had been holding it. His shoulders fell.

"Come inside."

Will hesitated for a moment and then followed him in. The house was exactly how he remembered it. There was something else though, an almost palpable sense of desolation in the place that hadn't been there before. A stink of loneliness permeated the walls.

Franklin walked straight into the kitchen, and Will heard him rattling around in the cupboards.

"You are nearly twenty now," he said from the kitchen. "Are you a whiskey man or a vodka man?"

"What makes you think I'm not a tequila man?"

"Only mongrels choose tequila as their favored drink, and no product of my family line is a mongrel." Franklin walked out with two glasses of vodka. "Whatever your linguistic preferences you are not a mongrel, Grandson, so I have chosen for you." He handed Will a glass. "You will be a vodka man."

Will took the glass and sat down in one of the chairs, his grandfather taking the seat across from him.

"You think that it is happenstance and that I just guess at these things, but I do not. I am a well-studied and informed student of human nature, Will. If I say a man will abuse his children, it is because of a certain exhibition of character or lack thereof that I have witnessed from him. If I say you are a vodka man, it is because you are and not because I simply wish it. People are not difficult to figure out."

"Is that why I have figured you out?" Will asked.

Franklin looked into his glass of vodka as if searching for an answer.

"On the front, this was one of our most valued possessions. I used to favor a fine German whiskey, but the fortunes of war changed that. We would raid Soviet positions and sack their supply units. Of course they were ripe with Russian and Ukrainian vodka, which we officers appropriated for ourselves."

"This was in between the mass slaughter of Jews?"

"For the most part." Franklin nodded casually and unapologetically as he sipped at his vodka. "You think I am a Devil."

"After a fashion." Will considered his words. "I find it difficult to reconcile my Grandfather with Franklin Hessler."

"Why is that? You never seemed to have any profound difficulty with this before. Suddenly something has changed?"

"I have learned things in years past. Or maybe the reality is still the same, but my perceptions have just changed."

"You are not seeing things through your German eyes." Franklin pointed at him.

"You don't have to see the world through Jewish eyes, Grandfather, to know when something is wrong."

"Wrong by whose definition, exactly?"

"A child's." Will paused and took a sip of his drink. It burned the back of his throat as he never was much of a drinker. "Even a child can look back at the Holocaust and understand that it was a horror beyond comprehension."

"You do not understand, you were not

there. The Jews and the Versailles treaty sought to break the back of Germany—"

"No one cares Grandfather!" Will snapped. "There's nothing you can say, nothing that is going to excuse the things you did. Nothing will remove their stain from history."

Outside the sky was overcast, and thunder split the silence between them.

"I know now, that this will not end well," Franklin said. He stood up slowly, and his age showed. He walked to the mantle where an array of family photographs sat. "Did I ever tell you about the report of angels, and what it means?"

"No, you didn't."

Franklin picked up a very old black and white framed photo. It was of his own father in uniform, waiting by a train to be sent to the front during World War One.

"I once asked my father, when I was a small child, what the thunder was. I asked him what beast made that sound and what it meant." Franklin smiled and set the picture down. "He told me that it was a sign that somewhere, something had gone wrong. He explained that when you shoot a rifle, the cracking sound is made by the speed of the traveling bullet breaking through the air, and that it is called a 'report.' My father had a strong belief in God, and that there were angels watching over all of us."

Franklin set the photo down and finished his glass of vodka.

"Do you know that he fought at Verdun... at the inferno? Half a million dead, and another million seriously wounded in ten months of the most savage fighting the world has ever known. My father told me that the angels that watch over us have fear just as man does, and that they can only bear so much. He told me that when the angels witness a horror on Earth that tears their hearts apart, they break away from it and return to Heaven for a time. He told me that when the angels flee the evil of man, they leave a report like that left by a speeding bullet, a report of angels."

Franklin sat back down in the chair across from Will.

"Perhaps that was the thunder we just heard, a report of angels." He looked at Will evenly for a moment. "I'm not going to see you again, am I?"

Will shook his head.

"I can't change who I am, William. My beliefs are not yours, and perhaps in time history will show that I was indeed wrong, but for now I cannot pretend to be something I am not."

"I understand that."

Will also understood that he was searching for something in his grandfather, hoping for something that wasn't there at all. It never had been.

CHAPTER 10

Will Hessler had not received the answers he wanted from his grandfather, despite pushing the man. What more was he supposed to say? Will had already as much as accused Franklin of murdering Irving, where was he to go that was further than that?

Franklin Hessler was very smart, smarter than the SFPD. He had brazenly murdered four men in the house on Balboa Avenue and gotten away with it without much trouble. Surely, he could murder one old man and not miss a step.

The bus ride home seemed to take forever, and Will sat in silence trapped with his own thoughts. The bus stopped in front of his apartment building and he walked out into a light rain. He jogged up the steps to his apartment, and after opening the door Will froze. Seeing the two of them in the same place was a shock to say the least.

Susanne sat on the couch with her head in her hands, and it was obvious that she had been crying. Isabelle stood against one of the walls with her arms folded across her stomach in a self-hugging motion, like she was trying to hold her emotions in. She had been crying as well.

Susanne looked up at Will as he stood in the doorway.

"Why are you doing this, Will?"

"What?"

It was the stupidest thing he could have possibly said, but at the time he couldn't think of anything else. Isabelle looked at Will and he could see that she felt trapped.

"I mean why haven't you called me in a week?" Susanne shouted. She put a hand to her forehead and let out a breath. "One week, Will, and I haven't seen or heard from you. I come here and she answers the door wearing your clothes. What in the hell is wrong with you?"

"I wasn't trying to hurt you," Will said quietly.

"Well you didn't do a very good job." Susanne stood up and walked around the room once. "I don't know what I did, Will, I really don't. What did I do that was so bad, so cruel that you did this to me, that you turned to her?"

"It's Isabelle, Susanne. I told you about her. I mean, it's not like she's a stranger."

"Are you insane? Is that supposed to make me feel better, that you've betrayed me with someone familiar?" Susanne shouted, and the walls seemed to tremble and withdraw. Her anger was shocking, but it should not have been. Will Hessler should have expected that this moment would come.

"What do you want me to say?" Will asked. "I mean- I don't feel good about this Susanne. It's nothing I wanted."

"Nothing you wanted?" she asked. "Nothing you wanted. That's just great Will, that makes me feel a lot better. Nothing you wanted. That's just great. Maybe I should just leave you and your girlfriend alone."

Will didn't say anything; he only stood there. What could he do, deny it?

Susanne picked up her purse and headed for the door. She stopped next to Will. He could see tears building up in her eyes but knew that she didn't want to cry in front of him.

"I would have done anything for you, and you ripped my heart out in return. I hope it's worth it."

She walked out and slammed the door.

There was a good minute of silence in the room. Will could hear Isabelle's breathing.

"I'm sorry, Will. I didn't know it was her at the door."

Will crossed the room and pulled her to him. He knew that she felt horrible about what had happened.

"I screw up everyone's lives, Will. Everywhere I go I ruin something. What's wrong with me?"

"It's not you, Isabelle, it's not your fault. Things will get better, I promise." Will held onto her like his life depended on it and whispered in Hebrew, "I'll make things better."

Two days later, Will saw it on the front page of

the San Francisco Chronicle and the headline hit him like a ton of bricks. The newspaper called him the day before asking for a comment on the release of his mother from prison and he had hung up on the reporter. It took seeing it in print for Will to fully grasp what was happening.

Sunset District Synagogue bomber released from prison.

There was a short statement from Diane Hessler's lawyer declaring that his client had justly been released from prison after reports of the police brutality used to coerce her confession had come to light. No one seemed to care that she had actually done it and that she had been responsible for all of those deaths.

How would Isabelle react to this news? Will waited in the quiet of the apartment for her to come back from the county hospital where she had gone for a follow-up examination.

Will still hadn't spoken to Susanne since the night before and had no real reason to expect her to ever reach out to him. They would not go on to become friends. They would not send each other Christmas cards. He could only imagine what she was feeling. Perhaps what he had felt when Isabelle dropped out of his life.

Susanne appealed to Will's rationale side, the part of him that wanted a normal life and a normal job, the part that wanted to know where his next meal was coming from and that he would always be loved.

What Susanne could not do for Will Hessler was understand the very nature of the engine that gave him purpose. He couldn't really talk to her about art because while she had a knowledge of art she didn't understand the meat of it, the unspoken emotions trapped beneath the strokes of paint on the canvas.

Isabelle could give Will those missing pieces.

A key turned in the lock of the apartment door, and Isabelle walked in with a bag of groceries she had picked up from the corner store.

"Isabelle, I have to tell you something."

She appeared in the kitchen door, eyes fixed on him.

"I already know, Will. I saw it in the papers this morning."

Will was quiet.

"I know I should feel something, but I don't. I only hope that she can go on with her life and I can go on with mine."

"Don't you hate her?"

Isabelle nodded.

"I'd like to say I'm all out of hate, but it's still there. It will be until the day I die, or these scars fade and my Grandmother comes back. I'm not going to let it rule my life though. That would make me like her. I have a second chance now, I'm not going to waste it."

Will nodded his understanding. He reached into his pocket and brought out a small box.

Isabelle watched as he opened it and removed a single item.

"You're getting better, Isabelle. You're healing," Will said as he hung the small Star of David around her neck. "Maybe this is part of that process. We'll go to Synagogue this Sunday, you and I. Okay?"

Isabelle nodded.

"I must . . ." She tugged at the sleeves of her sweater. She wore a stocking cap pulled down lower on the left side of her head than the right, giving her a somewhat motley appearance. "I must get a dress though, long sleeved. I- I need to wear long sleeves."

"You don't need to, Isabelle. You don't have to hide."

"My scars- I have to hide my scars."

Will rolled up her left sleeve, and she tried to pull her arm away. As her flesh was bared, she looked away from it. Will pulled off the stocking cap and kissed the side of her face, where it was reddish, and not as smooth as the rest of her flesh. He felt a tear roll across his lips.

"I have to hide my scars. You don't understand."

"I don't see your scars, Isabelle. I only see you."

Inspector Kellerman sat in his car for a long

time looking at Franklin Hessler's house. Irving Dyer had been missing for two weeks at that point, and not a single lead had turned up, not a thing. Normally SFPD would not have given nearly this much attention to one old man going missing, but John knew the backstory of this particular old man and that it was likely more than just a simple missing persons case. John couldn't prove that Franklin Hessler had anything to do with it, but his gut told him that the former Nazi officer was somehow involved.

It was the only thing that made sense. True, it seemed the two of them had been friendly, but there was the obvious factor of Franklin's daughter effectively murdering Irving Dyer's wife and injuring his granddaughter. How could Irving let that go? Had he finally confronted Hessler over the matter? Had they come to blows? Who could know?

So John decided to roust the old man and see what shook loose.

The house on Ortega seemed to be glaring at Inspector Kellerman, daring him to try something.

. . .

Franklin Hessler opened the door and didn't seem at all surprised to find Inspector Kellerman standing there.

"Good afternoon Inspector, how can I help you?"

"You mind if I come in?"

"Yes," Franklin Hessler said quickly, and then added, "I would like to know what this is about before I invite you into my home."

"I'm investigating the disappearance of Irving Dyer. You know him, correct?"

"Yes, in fact I am the one who reported him missing. The police at the time did not seem terribly concerned. Why the sudden fascination?"

"Sometimes it takes a while for things to work their way through the system. Now I'm here."

"Indeed. There are so many Inspectors working for the San Francisco Police Department though, it just strikes me as odd that you and your partner keep showing up at my door, bothering my family, digging up my garden in search of bodies that are not there."

"I know who you are, Hessler."

There was a perceptible shift in the air

between the two men. Franklin Hessler stood nearly a full foot taller than John Kellerman, and now he moved his right shoulder out a little, in a perhaps unconscious attempt to crowd the smaller man.

"Indeed?" Franklin could not resist a small smile tugging at the corners of his lips. "I did not know you read the art section of the newspaper."

"No, but I do read Interpol reports. I keep in touch with the Wiesenthal Center. We have connections with the Mossad. Do I have to keep going?"

"I'm not certain what you are getting at Inspector?"

"Don't play stupid with me, Hessler. Your problem, the thing that's going to take you out, is your arrogance. You think you're smarter than everybody else, but you're not. You killed innocent men, women, and children during the war, and I know that. If you were the one who went missing, I don't think anyone would come looking for you."

"Now you are threatening me? I see. What exactly is it, Inspector, that you think you know? Where is your proof? Hm?" Franklin leaned in closer, as if looking for the proof. "I see. Nothing. Shoot me, Inspector." He stepped back and held up his hands. "Right here, in broad daylight."

John Kellerman glared at Franklin. He could feel the blood pounding in his head.

"Ah, I see. All talk. Yes, Inspector," Franklin Hessler lowered his voice and leaned back in. "Yes, I did. Men, women, children. Lined up on the edge of the ditch, and then . . ." Franklin made an arcing motion with one of his long fingers. "Into the ditch full of holes and in piles. And I felt nothing, truly nothing. I used to target practice on Jewish women, because they were harder to hit with a pistol while they were running in terror, so unpredictable."

Kellerman slammed the door behind him and quickly closed the blinds. Outside the sun was going down. He looked at what he had done. Franklin Hessler was bleeding from his head and holding his stomach where John Kellerman had punched him. Hessler was obviously trying to say something, but the wind had been knocked out of him.

"Shit," Kellerman snapped as he paced around the room with his gun drawn.

"You . . . are finished," Franklin managed to get out.

"No!" Kellerman snapped and pointed the gun at Franklin. "You're fucking finished! You think I can do some shit like that and let you live? You think you're special? One more fucking Kraut I shoot in my lifetime, that's all." Kellerman pointed his revolver at Hessler and pulled back the hammer. "Nothing more."

"And what will you do with the body?"

Kellerman stopped. He looked Franklin in the eyes.

"I always had a plan," Franklin said, pulling out a handkerchief to wipe the blood from his face. "I always disposed of the bodies."

"I'll bury you in the park. It's big, plenty of room."

"And how, pray tell, will you get me out the door without the neighbors seeing? They're quite nosy. Just like an Irishman, all balls and no brains."

"What did you do with Dyer?"

Franklin Hessler sat up on the floor and

looked around. He spit some blood on the carpet.

"What did I do with Dyer? Irving?" Franklin looked at his handkerchief and grimaced at the amount of blood he found. He would need stitches where his head had met the butt of John Kellerman's pistol. "You mean how did I dispose of the body?"

Kellerman nodded.

"I buried him in a Jewish Cemetery, beside his wife in Colma. I had that much respect for my friend."

Kellerman shook his head.

"You are a bizarre old man. He was your friend!" Kellerman shouted, half in anger, half in disbelief. "How could you kill your friend? Especially after what your daughter did to his family?"

"Mercy!" Franklin Hessler roared. "You do not know what it was like to see him trying to be brave, acting so proud as if he felt nothing. Missing his Jew wife and granddaughter every day as if they could mean anything to anyone but him. I miss my goddamn dog from when I was nine, but I do not complain she is gone!"

Even John was stunned by this nonsensical line of logic.

"You don't get it, do you? You really don't understand."

"Understand what?"

"He wasn't acting you fool!" Kellerman snapped. "He was overcoming tragedy like he has been all of his life. Tragedy visited upon him by you and yours, and I don't believe for a second that you killed him out of some sense of brotherly compassion." Kellerman studied Hessler for a moment. "He figured you out, didn't he? All of that bullshit about Stalingrad was a lie. I never believed it and I'm betting he didn't either." Kellerman looked around the room. "What was it, what did he find?"

Franklin looked at the floor.

"Show me. Now."

Resigned to his fate, Franklin Hessler stood up, straightened himself out, and walked slowly to a box sitting on the mantle. For a short while he simply stood staring at it. A small brass lock gleamed on the latch.

"I had forgotten to replace the lock. Absent minded," Franklin Hessler said as he reached into his pocket and retrieved the key to the box with Kellerman standing behind him. "Age does that to you, you understand?"

Kellerman said nothing. Franklin fit the key into the lock and clicked it open.

He lifted the lid and looked inside.

"I . . . did not want to do it, but I had to. He found this."

Franklin took out a black-and-white photograph of himself and some other SS officers standing in a concentration camp. The four men in the photo seemed to be in good spirits. One held a bottle of wine.

"You killed your friend because he found out who you really were," Kellerman whispered, looking at the photo.

"Most often, Inspector, I find that it is curiosity which kills the kittens."

Inspector John Kellerman looked up in time to see the last thing he ever would.

Will Hessler had not seen Inspector Stein since his mother's trial, so at first he didn't recognize the policeman who walked into the art gallery where Will worked. Ronald had cut his hair much shorter and put on a few pounds since then. There was also something else different about him. It was almost a sense of premature age, and something about his eyes. It might seem odd to say, but it was as if he knew the date and time that the world was to conclude yet was required to remain silent about it.

"William Hessler?" he asked.

"Yes. Inspector Stein, correct?"

He nodded and shook Will's hand.

"You don't read the papers much, do you? Crime beat section?"

"Inspector, I have to admit I don't know what you're talking about."

From his inside suit pocket, Ronald pulled a folded newspaper page and handed it to Will. He opened it up and read the article. It was about a missing San Francisco Police Inspector whose body had been found buried next to the buffalo in Golden Gate Park. An anonymous party had seen a man burying something in the park late at night and reported it as seeming suspicious.

It was Inspector Kellerman. John. John was dead. Someone had killed John. Franklin Hessler had killed John. Will knew it right away.

"Do you know why I'm here, Will?" Ronald asked.

Will hesitated before looking up and nodding.

"John called me the day before he disappeared. We don't work together anymore, but he wanted to review your mother's case with me. He was under orders to stay away from her, but I could tell he wasn't going to let it go. It seems he was working on a missing persons case, a guy named Irving Dyer. Turns out your mom killed this guy Irving's wife in the bombing. Have you seen her since her release?"

"Um... no. She hasn't tried to contact me."

Ronald rubbed his face with one hand and looked around the gallery. His eyes were bloodshot, and he hadn't shaved in a few days. Something was eating him alive inside.

"Will, somebody killed John. I mean okay that's obvious. The way it was done though, at close range with a nine-millimeter, execution style in the forehead. Then he gets buried in the park. This wasn't some random thing, you see. This was personal. There were plenty of people out there that would have liked to do

John in, but not many who could have done it like that."

"And you think my mother did it?"

"She has the motive, and it's the same way those people were killed back on Balboa before the bombing. At the time we liked your grandfather for it, but she makes a hell of a lot more sense, and the timing can't be ignored."

"Inspector, I just don't... I don't think my mother has the patience to pull something like this off. She's less like a surgeon and more like a sledgehammer."

There was something about the way Will was standing there, or the way he was acting, or maybe something in his eyes. He knew that Inspector Stein was aware he knew something but was afraid to say it directly.

"This is a difficult situation, Will, I am aware of that, but you have to know I'm going to figure this out."

"Doesn't my mom have to check in with a parole officer or something? Can't you get a hold of her that way?"

Ronald shook his head.

"Her conviction was overturned, there's no parole officer, no nothing. In fact, her lawyer is suing the courts for compensation for the time she did."

"So, you had her dead to rights bombing a synagogue, but she gets off scot-free?"

"I don't like it any more than you do," Ronald snapped.

Will looked around the gallery and saw that it was pretty much empty. He wanted to be able to say he had to help a customer and couldn't talk anymore. He felt as guilty as hell knowing that his grandfather may have killed John Kellerman, but stating this was something he was not ready for.

"Let me talk to a couple of people, Inspector, see if I can find out anything about where my mother is."

Inspector Stein looked skeptical.

"You'd be willing to sell your mother down the river?"

"It sounds bad when you say it like that."

"Sometimes doing the right thing doesn't feel so good. Sometimes it makes you feel like shit. I get that."

For the first time, it occurred to Will Hessler that one of his family members could conceivably kill him if he became further involved in this.

"I have a problem, Isabelle."

Setting down the book she was reading Isabelle looked up from the small table in what passed for a kitchen in Will's apartment.

"What is it, Will?"

"I think my Grandfather killed a cop, a friend of mine."

"Did you tell the police?"

"No, not yet." Will hesitated, unsure how he should say what was on his mind. "It's hard for me. I know that he's bad, I know that now but I still care for him."

"Will, I understand. Maybe this sounds stupid, but I don't hate your mother, or your grandfather."

"How? After what they've both done?"

Isabelle seemed to think about it for a moment and then shook her head.

"It's been burned out of me, in more ways than one. I don't have any room in my life for hatred, I've got too much to rebuild. I'm not going to tell you to turn in your grandfather.

You do what you think is right, but don't do it because you're worried about what I will think. Whatever may happen today or tonight, tomorrow will still come."

Despite the confusion swirling about his life, Will Hessler knew that Isabelle was right.

"First off, you and I are done. Do you understand?"

Will had entered under false pretenses. He didn't want to do it on the doorstep, so he waited until he was inside to give it to his grandfather with both barrels.

"Fine. I do not care. You and I are not going to see eye to eye; I understand that. We had some good years together, but that is history."

Franklin Hessler was visibly agitated.

"What did you do to Inspector Kellerman?"

Despite knowing that his grandson was smart, and would likely soon root out all of the family secrets, Franklin was surprised by this question.

"I do not know what you are talking about. What are you talking about? Have you gone insane?"

Franklin turned away from Will and was walking toward the kitchen. Will took him by the shoulder and spun him around.

"Don't walk away from me, you tell me what you did!" he shouted.

"Have you lost your mind?"

"Do you think I am stupid Grandfather? Do you?"

"No- I don't- you do not understand!" he shouted back, his voice booming. "I love her! I cannot..." his voice trailed off, and he looked at the floor.

Then and there Will knew where his mother had been. He understood where she had disappeared to after her release from prison.

"She's been here," Will said quietly. "Did she?"

Franklin nodded. He slowly walked across the room and collapsed into a chair.

"I cannot betray her. I cannot."

"She killed him."

Franklin seemed afraid to look his grandson in the eye.

"You're both mad."

"You do not understand because you are so

Americanized. Your mother and I are divergent in our beliefs, but there is still a common thread to bind us. You have always been like this stranger who lives among us."

"So, I am a stranger then, but you must turn her in."

"I will not."

"Why did she have to kill him?" Will asked, switching gears.

Franklin took his time removing a cigarette from his small aluminum case and lit it between his lips. He inhaled deeply and let a smooth cloud of smoke roll out of his mouth to spread across the ceiling.

"The Inspector came here looking for information about Irving Dyer. We had a confrontation. He would most certainly have killed me had your mother not caved his skull in with a lamp."

Will was afraid to ask the question.

"Did you kill Irving Dyer?"

His grandfather stared at him and then nodded.

"Why?" Will shouted and shook, feeling tears rolling down his face. "What is wrong with you? Why?"

"He found me out. He would have reported me or killed me himself. I only did unto him... before he had a chance to do unto me."

"And all of that time and your friendship to him, they mean nothing to you?"

"They mean nothing!" he snapped back. "Self-preservation, my Grandson, is a virtue you have not had to exercise, so do not lecture me as to the evils of its use! He was my friend, I took his life, and it means nothing to me!"

"I'm calling the Wiesenthal center."

The wind went out of Franklin Hessler, and his shoulders slumped slightly as his spirit lost some of its rigidity.

"Was it that horrible?" Franklin asked, conversationally.

"The murders?"

"Your upbringing."

Will studied the old man closely.

"Not horrible, perhaps bearable. There were good things. I imagine you did your best with what you had, what you knew."

Franklin opened a small gilded box on the table next to his chair. He removed a pistol and sat it down on his knee. For a brief moment,

Will was horrified to think his grandfather may actually kill him.

"You must believe that I am sorry for the bad things. In the end I suppose my desire for self-preservation, my 'virtue' was greater than my ability to be a father or a grandfather." He tapped the pistol with a long finger. "Now leave me to what I must do, the one gift I can give you."

"What will you do?"

"Leave me!" Franklin roared, and the intensity of his command propelled Will out of the house and down the front steps like a physical being pushing him. Will let the door slam shut behind him, and he stood on the lawn for a moment staring at the house before walking away.

Isabelle slept, and Will sat by the phone thinking. He really was going to call Wiesenthal's people. Would he be selling his soul in some way? If so, then to whom? Will thought over what his Grandfather had done before he left the house. Did he intend to take his own life with that pistol, or someone else's? It was hard to judge the man. Would he allow himself to be captured, or go all the way to hell in order to escape what would be waiting for him in Israel? For Franklin Hessler, it was not so much the prospect of prison as having to be accused by those "people" and being made to answer to them.

For the longest time Will sat and watched Isabelle sleep. He knew he had to protect her, but he didn't know how.

Will lay down next to Isabelle and stared at her. Her breathing changed, and her eyes opened.

"Are you watching me sleep?" she asked.

Will smiled.

"Will, do you trust me?"

"Of course. Why do you ask?"

Isabelle bit her lower lip.

"Sometimes people do things you don't understand, stuff that feels bad."

"Are you talking about... when you wouldn't talk to me?"

Isabelle looked away.

"Maybe. Just... sometimes..." Her voice drifted off, and she closed her eyes. "Goodnight Will."

Her hand gripped his.

Will woke hours later to the sound of someone knocking hard on his apartment door. He was half asleep walking to the door and opened it.

In a half a second, he was more awake than he had ever been.

"Why didn't you tell me where you lived?"

She didn't look insane. Her eyes were narrowed, but still happy at seeing him. It had been a year since Will last saw her, and the passage of time had taken its toll on his mother. The lines on her face were more pronounced and her beauty had been dulled by hours behind bars and hidden from the light.

"Because I didn't want you to find me. Please leave," Will said flatly, coldly.

She looked distraught.

"I don't... I don't understand. Your grandfather told me you had changed, he said you would not want to see me, but I didn't believe it!"

"He was right! I don't want to see you! Or him! I want you to stay away from me!"

"What did I do that was so bad, Will? Can

you tell me that?" she pleaded. "I did everything I could as a mother, everything I could to
raise you right and give you every advantage!"

"Are you mad?" Will snapped. "You blew
up a synagogue! What do you mean you don't
know what you did? Let me spell this out for
you; you are insane, and you need to stay away
from me!"

Her eyes began tearing up and her lips
trembled. She didn't understand.

"That had nothing to do with you! With us!
That was for me, not you!"

It was a dull thumping sound that Will did
not immediately identify for what it was. He
reached back and threw Isabelle to the floor
before he even realized who she was and what
she had done. It was enough force to leave her
dazed as Diane Hessler tumbled back against
the door with the kitchen knife buried in her
chest.

"Will, I'm sorry! I'm sorry! I'm sorry!"
Isabelle screamed over and over as she looked
up at him.

In the small room the shots sounded like
thunder. One of the bullets grazed Will's calf
and sent him to the floor. He came face to face

with his mother as she fired the pistol at Isabelle, the rounds digging into the girl's chest and shoulders, including the one that had nicked Will, mixing their blood. Will scrambled to Isabelle, trying to put his body between her and his mother's aim.

There was another crash in the room, followed by a loud grunt and a sick cracking sound as Franklin Hessler stomped on Diane's hand. He fell to one knee and clamped his hands over her mouth and nose.

Franklin looked over his shoulder at Will and shouted, "Look away boy! Now!"

Will obeyed his Grandfather's command and heard his mother's legs kicking as she suffocated. He could only imagine that Franklin was looking into his daughter's eyes and praying for her as she died.

Isabelle stared up at Will, her chest covered with blood. Her hand reached out and gripped his.

"I'm sorry, Will, I should have told you," her voice gurgled as her lungs filled with blood.

"Don't say anything." Will crawled over her and tried to hold her still as she started to shake.

"I lied to you, Will. It was all so I could get back at her! I'm sorry!"

"Shut up! Don't say anything. Please don't say it."

Isabelle's eyes were filled with tears and she sobbed as her breathing became more fluid and labored.

"It's important to me. It's important that you know the truth. I love you, I do. In the beginning I didn't, but now I do, and I have to leave you—"

"You're not dying," Will whispered, but her chest had already stopped moving. Isabelle's eyes were fixed on his, but there was no spark behind them.

"No." It was more of a low, sorrowful howl than anything human.

Will sat up and put his hands on his face. He pulled them away and saw Isabelle's blood on them. His hands were shaking.

"I am sorry." It was Franklin, sitting against the wall with his daughter's pistol in his hand. She was dead. "More than you can ever know."

Will cried sitting over Isabelle's body. The gears of his universe were grinding against each other and tearing his world apart.

"How did this happen?" was all Will could think to ask. He really did not know where he was or what had happened.

"I'm sorry. I thought... I thought I would be in time."

"You were not."

In the distance Will heard sirens wailing through the air.

"They are coming," Franklin said. He checked the chamber of the pistol for a round and held it out to Will. "I cannot allow myself to be taken, and I cannot do this to myself."

Will stared at him in disbelief.

"Go to hell."

Franklin's face fell, and he took the pistol in his hands, resting it in his lap. He looked at Isabelle.

"I remember, when she was a girl, and you were a boy. The two of you painting in my garden. Everything was simpler then. I didn't have to think about the things I had done, or the possible repercussions that would come tomorrow. I lived in the moment, and the moment was quite fine. I did not understand that my daughter was becoming a monster before my unseeing eyes. I curse now the hour and the day that she was born. All of the pain, all of the destruction she has brought to everyone she touched."

Will said nothing. Now he was holding Isabelle in his arms. He couldn't let her go, even though she was already gone.

Franklin looked away from Will and to the doorway, to the sound of the police cars coming. Tears were rolling down his cheeks.

"I will give you then, the only gift I can."

He put the gun in his mouth and Will turned away. It was a loud pop like a cap gun. It was a loud pop like the end. Will looked from the blood on his hands, to the blood on the wall behind his Grandfather's head, to the blood on the floor that was flowing out of his calf. He had lost a lot of blood, and slowly the room blurred until he passed out.

Will Hessler awoke in a world of numbness wrapped in white. For a few blissful moments, he couldn't remember what had happened, and then it came flooding back to him.

"How are you feeling?"

Will's vision was a little blurred as he came

out of his coma-like sleep, but he recognized Inspector Stein standing by the door with a cup of coffee in his hand. The man looked like he hadn't slept in days. He looked like a mess. He looked like Will felt.

Will didn't say anything. He didn't want to hear what had happened after he passed out. He wanted to believe that somehow Isabelle had pulled through even though he had watched her die in his arms.

Ronald Stein walked across the room and stood over him. He sat a second paper cup filled with coffee on the table beside Will's bed.

"I'm not a hundred percent sure if you're supposed to be drinking that stuff, but it probably won't kill you."

Will propped himself up in bed and took a sip from the cup. He didn't normally drink coffee, but it seemed like as good a time as any to start.

"You know?" Ronald asked quietly.

Will nodded.

"They say that... she probably didn't feel anything. I mean, the way that it... the way that it happened she may have been conscious, but she was numb."

Will was not sure what to say to that, or what comfort those words were supposed to hold for him.

"What about the others? My mother?" Will asked.

"Dead. Do you remember what happened?"

"Yes."

Ronald pulled out a chair and sat down. Reaching out with his foot, he kicked the door shut. Will watched the Police Inspector light a cigarette. He saw Will looking at him and shrugged.

"If none of this other bullshit's going to kill you, this probably won't either."

"I'm sorry about John," Will said.

"I'm sorry about your family."

"Do you think it's me?" Will asked.

Ronald looked at Will with a squint.

"You? What do you mean?"

"Everyone around me dies violently."

Ronald thought on it for a moment.

"It's not you, it's them. People set themselves up for stuff sometimes. The family you were born into is not your fault." Ronald stood up and walked around the bed. "You loved her, didn't you?"

Will nodded.

"I did. I can't believe she's gone. I can't believe it."

Ronald's fingers were tapping the safety rail on one side of the bed in a rhythmic motion. He was chewing on his lip. Will could sense something was eating at him.

"What is it?" Will asked. He was afraid of what Ronald would tell him.

"There's a girl. She found out you were here, and she's been sacked out in the lobby ever since."

Will knew who she was, but he asked anyway.

"Who is she?"

"Susanne Bonafide. Her father's here too, he was raising hell because the hospital staff wouldn't let them see you. I don't fuck around with Marine Colonels, so I let them in. The girl was sitting next to your bed crying for quite a while." Ronald stubbed his cigarette out on the bottom of his shoe and dropped it in a waste-basket. "She cares about you a lot."

"I know."

"Look, Will, I don't know if it means much after all that's happened, but if you ever want to talk, or just... whatever, give me a call." Ronald dropped his card on the bedside table. "You and I have a lot in common after all of this. We've both lost folks, lost blood, lost family."

Will looked at him with a little surprise.

"I lost someone in the synagogue," Ronald said quietly. He walked toward the door and looked over his shoulder. "Susanne will want to come in."

Susanne walked in without saying a word and sat down beside Will's bed. He felt so uncomfortable, not from the gunshot wound but from the silence between them. It was like an animal sitting there quietly chewing on bits of their past.

"I'm sorry, Will. I think... I don't know what to say."

"I'm sorry, Susanne."

"What are you sorry for?"

"The way I treated you. I should have handled it better."

"Will, I know you don't have much experience with this. I mean with relationships. You were scared, I understand that."

"It's no excuse though."

"No, it's not. The thing that really upset me, wasn't necessarily finding Isabelle there." Susanne rubbed her forehead. "Will, you were supposed to be the one who would stand by me no matter what, and then all of a sudden you were gone. I felt like I was abandoned."

Will remained silent, knowing that nothing he could say would change the way she was feeling. It would most likely just upset her more.

"Maybe now things can be different for you though. Don't get me wrong, Will, what happened was horrible, but maybe... I'm sorry."

"What?"

"It just sounds horrible. To say that now that your family is dead, you can try to be who you really are, instead of what they wanted you to be."

"I was never what they wanted me to be."

"But you spent so much time fighting it that you were never really what you wanted to be either. You know that."

"I do."

Susanne stood up and looked around the room. Her lower lip trembled.

"Will, I feel like an idiot saying this. I know you think I'm pathetic."

"Susanne, I don't think that."

"I'll wait for you, Will," she said, cutting him off. "I'll wait for you to come back to me because I think there's still something between us. I know you don't, but I do. Maybe in a while things will be different."

Will remained silent. Susanne leaned in and kissed his forehead, one of her tears splashing against his cheek.

She walked out of the room and closed the door.

Will Hessler was alone again.

CHAPTER 11

"You look broken."

Will Hessler did not think he was that easy to read, but it appeared he was wrong, at least where Mary Gauss was concerned.

It had been months since the death of his mother, grandfather and Isabelle. He had wanted to go back to Susanne, to bury his pain in her embrace, but he was afraid of what the result would be. What he said to Ronald Stein was true; everyone around him died violently. The ones that didn't seemed to survive only as broken souls wandering in purgatory.

He did not want to visit that fate upon Susanne Bonafide.

"What makes you think that?" Will asked as they sat in the bar on Haight Street.

"You're easy to read." Mary leaned forward, her left leg wrapped around his. "Didn't you see me sitting here?"

"Yes," Will answered.

"Why didn't you say something? Were you afraid?"

"But not for the reasons you might think."

"You weren't afraid of rejection," she said, taking a sip of her beer. "You fear what lies at the end of the road."

"I haven't even stepped foot on the road, so I suppose I shouldn't be so presumptuous."

"It doesn't hurt to be cautious."

"I suppose not."

Mary leaned forward and kissed Will Hessler, just minutes after they had met, but he sensed a connection there, and a softness that he had rarely felt, a familiar softness that was powerful enough to break down the walls of solitude he had built.

Mary was a smoking, drinking, rebellious poet who seemed simultaneously to have a great love and disdain for life. She lovingly destroyed everything she touched, and while Will Hessler could sense that he was on her hit list he did not care. At that moment in time he needed some sort of connection.

Mary tried as hard as she could to build trust between the two of them, but whatever was inside of Will that should have allowed for that was broken. He wanted to let her in, but it wasn't happening. Despite that she stayed around.

"I know that you're going to hurt me," she said, and kissing Will bit his lip as she pulled away, "But I know how to hit back, so it's okay."

Will went back to work at the gallery, and began attending San Francisco City College, though he wasn't quite sure why. It just seemed like the thing to do.

Most evenings Will stayed with Mary. She cooked his meals and watched over him as he slept. In many ways she seemed to be his guardian angel. He never revealed anything of his past to her. When Mary probed, Will told her that his parents had died, but never mentioned the how of it. She asked him about past girlfriends and he spoke of Susanne Bonafide, but never of Isabelle Dyer.

In those months, there was another bombing in the Sunset District. It was a small one in a kosher deli Will and Isabelle had frequented in days gone by. Seven people were killed, one of whom was an unborn child. No one claimed responsibility for it and soon reports began to circulate that it was a gas explosion. Either way, the incident brought memories of Will's past back to the surface in bold relief and plunged him into a depression that lasted for several weeks, but one from which he did recover.

It was a cool winter afternoon, and Will arrived at the gallery a half hour early to do his prep work before starting his shift. He was late far too often, and had decided that he needed to get his act together if he wanted to keep his job.

After much conversation on the subject with the owner Mister Reinhold, it was decided that they could leave the door propped open on occasion to air the place out without too much concern of the salt air damaging the paintings.

It was because the door was propped open that Will did not hear the older man enter, and did not notice him until he was already upon him.

This man was short and stocky, with thick black-framed glasses and a way of carrying himself that implied he was a man of some means. He stood at the end of the gallery observing a single painting that hung beneath a light. This painting (much like the open door) was a matter of some discussion. It was one of the few remaining works of the late Franklin Hessler and was in fact owned by Will Hessler.

The painting was a portrait of the Hessler family, such as they were. Franklin, Diane and Will sitting and smiling for the unseen artist. It was a lie.

"It's not for sale," Will said as he walked across the gallery. "Sorry. We should really take it down."

"It's quite good. Beautiful, in a way," the man said.

"I guess it depends on which side of the painting you're on."

The man turned to Will and smiled.

"My name is Saul Greenbaum," he said.

"Will Hessler," Will offered.

"I know who you are, Mister Hessler. Everyone knows who you are."

"I'm not sure how I feel about that," Will said. Looking over his shoulder he noticed a tall man with dark hair and a beard standing in front of the gallery window, looking in at them. "Friend of yours?"

"Jacob is just being cautious," Saul said. "It's his job."

"What job is that?"

"We find things. Things that don't want to be found."

"Such as?"

"People like your mother and your grandfather."

Will paused for a moment, unsure how to respond to that.

"And what do you do with them when you find them?"

"We don't bake them a birthday cake, I will tell you that much."

Saul walked to the gallery desk, took a pencil and a piece of paper and scrawled some words on it before handing it to Will.

Will turned the paper over in his hand and read it.

. . .

Nazi Hunters.

"Like Wiesenthal?" Will asked.

Saul smiled.

"He is a friend. We are more... official in nature."

The Mossad.

"Look, Mister Greenbaum, this is all very interesting, but did you come here to see me specifically?"

"From what I understand, you are something of a rarity. You speak English, German, Spanish and Hebrew, all fluently."

"I don't know if I'd say fluently."

"And you already have operational experience. More importantly, the media did you quite a dis-service by implying that you were somehow aware of your mother's plans to bomb the synagogue."

"That was bullshit!" Will snapped. It was true, the Chronicle in particular had done a hatchet job on him.

"Bullshit perhaps, but fortunate in a way.

You may eventually be approached by people who think you are of a like mind." Saul could read the confusion on Will's face. "The burgeoning neo-Nazi movement, Mister Hessler, will be very interested in you."

"No one has tried to recruit me, if that's what you're asking."

"When they come, you will not know it. That is how they operate. They secret themselves into your life, and by the time you realize who and what they are, you are one of them."

"You make it sound like getting cancer."

"It's not that different."

"Mr. Greenbaum, I'm barely out of high school. I mean... okay, so I speak a few languages, but come on. I really think you've got the wrong guy. I mean, what is it you're even asking me to do?"

"There is a shortage of men who can walk between worlds, and that is what we need. It's not just about the white power groups. We need someone who can infiltrate American offshoots of groups like Black September, DFLP, and other Fatah branches."

"I'm sorry, Mr. Greenbaum, but you have the wrong person for this."

"Will, do not make such a summary judgment. At least consider it."

"There is nothing to consider," Will said sharply. "You have made a mistake."

Will turned and walked away. Saul touched his arm, not to stop him, but to draw his attention.

"Will, please. I will respect your decision." Will turned to look at Saul. "At least take my card. If you ever want to talk."

Will took the card and put it in his pocket if for no other reason than to make Saul leave him alone.

"I don't really have anything to say," Will said.

Saul nodded and walked away.

"Do you know what you need, Will?" Mary asked, breaking him out of his thoughts as they sat at dinner.

Will smiled and shook his head.

"You need to get out of this city for a while. Maybe down to Santa Cruz or somewhere. Maybe even Mexico!"

"Mexico?" The idea was as foreign to him

as… well, Mexico.

"Sure. Some friends of mine are going down there this weekend. We can hitch a ride with them and just have a good time."

"I don't know, Mary. I've got work."

"Will, you can't not go. You're going to break in half if you don't relax a little. Besides, I don't think you can honestly give me a good reason why you can't go."

Will stared at her for a moment and shrugged. She was right. He needed to disconnect from San Francisco and all of the ghosts walking its streets.

Mary's friends were like night and day. You could not track down two more different people. Maxwell seemed like the typical California surfer type, laid back and without a care in the world. Will suspected that Maxwell had no idea how much money was in his wallet. Randall, on the other hand, did not speak much at all aside from a polite introduction when they first met. Will could tell that Randall was very, very serious. He was dressed in some sort of pseudo military uniform, all black and without any frills.

The four of them piled into the fifty-nine DeSoto and began what Will believed would be a rather arduous journey to Mexico.

Gradually Will got to know Max and Randall better and even managed to pry a couple of full sentences out of Randall. Will knew that they were both very protective of Mary, so he was being watched with a critical eye.

Will had never been out of the United States before, aside from that first flight from Argentina when he was five, when Eichmann was captured and they had fled. Crossing the border from San Diego into Mexico felt like a fairly big event, but at the same time there did not seem to be a perceptible difference between Southern California and Mexico. It was basically a lot of desert.

They stopped in Tijuana for dinner, but after that promptly got back on the road and headed out. Will assumed they would spend their time in one of the towns he had heard of like Rosarito or Camino Verde, but it soon became obvious that they were not heading to either of those places.

The four drove straight through the night in the DeSoto, burning gasoline and desert miles. Sometime around midnight Randall took over driving responsibilities from Will after he had strayed off course several times, which made sense, as he had no idea where he was going and was in a desert. It must have been something about being behind the wheel in Mexico that brought Randall to life. He began talking about everything from the fall of the Roman Empire to Roosevelt's New Deal. He somehow managed to interject the teachings of Karl Marx into everything, normally as the cure all that would have fixed whatever problem was present. Will didn't bother questioning any of Randall's theories as he figured it would be best not to stir him up too much.

"Shit!"

Will sat bolt upright in his seat as Randall hit the brakes and the car skidded to a stop in the dust. Maxwell and Mary both slammed into the backs of the front seats.

"What the fuck, Randall?" Mary shouted, rubbing her forehead.

"Sorry, I'm sorry! I almost missed it! Blame Rollo, he's the asshole who picked a town with three buildings in it to do the pick up!"

"Who's an asshole?" a voice with a thick Russian accent growled out of the darkness beside the car.

"Jesus!" Randall shouted, jumping in his seat. "Don't do that!"

Roland Federov stepped closer to the car and leaned in the window.

"You fuckers are late."

"In case you hadn't noticed there's about a thousand miles of ink black desert out here to navigate through, so don't give us any shit, Rollo," Mary snapped.

Rollo's face went blank, then immediately turned to something approximating anger when he noticed Will Hessler.

"Who the fuck is that?"

"That's Will, Mary's squeeze," Maxwell said.

"Well, did anyone bother to check this asshole out, or did blind love bring him down here?"

"Shut up, Rollo, he's cool," Mary snapped at him.

"We'll see."

Rollo walked around to the front of the car, and before Will recognized what was happening, Rollo had opened the passenger side door and yanked Will out onto the ground. He rebounded fairly quickly and started to get up, only to find himself looking down the barrel of a gun.

Everyone else was out of the car, yelling at Rollo to put the gun down. Rollo responded by turning the gun on them. Will's ears were ringing, and he realized the Rollo had probably hit him with something after pulling him out of the car.

"All of you shut the fuck up!" Rollo yelled in an authoritative tone that did serve to silence everyone. He was no longer an equal; he was running the show. That much was clear. "I know you're a bunch of stupid college kids, but you're messing with my machine! I can't believe you bring this guy down here without bothering to take the time to find out if he's some nigger loving cop!"

It was jarring to Will to hear him say that. It was like getting slapped in the face. As if being on his knees in the middle of the desert at night with this Russian psycho holding a gun to his head wasn't bad enough, Will had the creeping feeling Rollo was of the same stock his mother had been. Will knew this because for the first time since Rollo had surfaced, he had the opportunity to get a clear view of the Iron Eagle grasping the Swastika tattooed on his right bicep.

"Tell him you're not a cop, Will," Mary shouted.

"I'm not a cop," Will said.

Rollo looked at Will hard for a moment as if evaluating with some internal lie detector whether or not this was the truth. Rollo's left eye twitched, and he tightened his grip on the pistol.

"Are you a nigger lover?" Rollo said, sounding out the words as if Will may not be totally clear on just what they meant. Will's mind was a blank, and he just stared at him. He wasn't sure how to approach the question, and had a suspicion that it didn't really matter how he responded.

"Give me your wallet," Rollo said, holding out his hand.

"Rollo, he's not a cop, knock it off," Mary said from behind him.

"Shut your mouth. I want to know just who this fucker is."

Rollo gestured with his fingers for Will to hand him his wallet.

The wallet with Saul Greenbaum's card in it.

Will Hessler figured that he was dead either way.

"You know what?" Will said, standing up and pressing his forehead to the muzzle of the gun. "Shoot me. You think I'm a nigger lover? Then shoot me. If you think turning on each other like a bunch of Jews is going to help, then go ahead and shoot me." His mother's words were coming out of his mouth. Will felt his stomach turn and hoped he could keep himself from vomiting.

Rollo glared at him. For a moment Will thought it was really over, and then the Russian lowered his gun and put it back in the holster.

"Sorry, no hard feelings? It seems that the police are everywhere in your country. I'm a little suspicious." Rollo held out his hand. "Justifiably so, I think."

"Well, fortunately we're not in my country at the moment."

Rollo laughed at that, a dark and gravelly laugh that imparted the same sense of joy a psychotic child would have in strangling his first cat.

"I'm sorry, Will. I had no idea that was going to happen."

Mary was close to tears as they stood some ways away from the car. Maxwell, Randall, and Rollo were a few dozen feet further away discussing something in hushed tones. They had hauled a crate out of a locked shed and loaded it into the trunk of the DeSoto.

"What is this? Who is he?" Will asked. He still had no idea what was going on.

"Rollo kind of... does things," Mary said with some hesitation.

"What things?"

"Things other people don't want to get caught doing."

"What things?" Will repeated.

"Look, Will, I don't even know everything. I only know what they tell me. I'm just here because I want to be involved, because I think it's important to be able to tell my grandkids I at least tried to do something, that I didn't just sit around and watch it happen."

"Watch what happen?" Will was growing tired of the riddles.

Mary stared at him for a moment as if she were psychically trying to unlock his thoughts.

"We're on the same side, me and you. I just don't know if you're ready to take it to the same level we are." Mary took his hands in hers. "Are you?"

It suddenly dawned on Will what she was getting at, and it hit him with the force of an all too familiar hammer. He remembered Saul Greenbaum's words in the gallery.

"When they come, you will not know it."

It all made sense. She had targeted him because of what the Chronicle wrote about him and what his mother had done. She was recruiting him.

"You're talking about the Jewish problem," Will said.

Mary nodded.

"The Jews, the niggers, the spics, all of them. They're not supposed to be here," she said plaintively, and it did not escape Will's attention that they were standing in Mexico. "We want to finish the work your mother started, and your grandfather before her and my own grandfather. I'm not sure about the timeline, but we want to make these people understand they can't just walk all over us, that they can't take our country. We need someone like you, who speaks Hebrew and German, who can walk between both worlds."

She was using Saul Greenbaum's same pitch.

"The group needs me, or you need me?"

"Both." She looked into Will's eyes. "I need you."

Mary leaned in and kissed him. It was all Will could do to hold his dinner down and restrain his body's desire to pull back.

"That is all you know?"

Will looked up from his coffee at Saul and winced at the seeming ingratitude.

"I'm sorry I didn't ask more questions while I was on my knees in the Mexico desert with a gun to my head."

Saul seemed unmoved by Will's complaint.

"I would like to know what was in that crate," Saul said.

Inspector Stein sat next to Saul, not saying much. Will had called Ronald after he returned to San Francisco and asked him to join the meeting. While Will had no reason to believe Saul was anything other that what he claimed to be, bringing Ronald in on it seemed like the smart play.

"It might be hard to find out what's in it. They don't fully trust me." Will paused. "Not yet."

"But you are already inside," Saul said.

"Yes, I am inside." Will thought about it. "I'm just saying that I can't be really obvious about my intentions. This has to move very slowly. So I don't get my head blown off."

"That is understandable, William. I would not want you to think that your personal safety is not a concern."

"I've done some undercover work, Will," Ronald interjected. "It's not enough for you to take it slowly or be careful. You have to be an Oscar caliber actor. It's important to me that you understand how dangerous this is."

"I understand, Inspector."

Ronald stared at Will, and it was obvious that the inspector had serious misgivings about the whole adventure.

"Now, William," Saul began, "My organization is experiencing a transitional phase at the moment, attempting to learn how to deal with these new threats."

"What Saul is trying to say, Will, is that he can't just kidnap these kids out of the country or take them in an alley and shoot them in the back of the head."

"Nazi Hunting is simpler in some ways," Saul said, continuing as if he had not been interrupted. "With these new groups we are really operating out of our approved area, so to speak. Police and government agencies that have looked the other way over the past thirty years may not continue to do so if we are conducting operations that they feel are interfering with their 'sovereign rights.' We cannot allow ourselves to become at odds with them. In order to avoid this potential problem, we are simply going to be doing the legwork and turning the case over to the authorities, to include Interpol."

"That's where I come in," Ronald said. "You'll be working with me as well as Saul. Your job is only to collect information, not to take action of any kind. In the event you get into trouble and are able to, you call me."

"And if I'm not able?" It was the first thing that popped into Will's mind.

"Hopefully that will not be the case," Saul interjected.

"But it could be."

Saul nodded.

"These kids have more to lose than the traditional Nazi groups. You saw that firsthand with your grandfather. If he was captured, it would have meant death for him, so he thought nothing of doing whatever was necessary in order to evade capture. There was no reasoning with him. These kids are different in that even if they are captured, they most likely will be looking at a short jail term, if that. They're less likely to go on a killing spree to avoid capture."

"Not Rollo," Will said. After having that psycho hold a gun to his head, there was no way these two were going to convince Will that the Russian was as harmless as a lamb.

Ronald looked at Saul. Will had a strong

suspicion that there was something they were not telling him.

"What is it?" Will asked. "What do you know about Rollo?"

"We wanted to wait until we knew if it was actually him," Ronald began. "We still don't know for sure, but it makes sense. Roland Federov escaped from a Soviet prison over a year ago and just vanished. He had been caught trying to buy explosives from a Red Army Officer. Prior to that, Roland was loosely affiliated with the Democratic Front for the Liberation of Palestine, but nothing as in depth as the KGB's affiliation with Black September."

"Young Roland," Saul began, "Found the perfect marriage of Jew hating and a Marxist political structure in the DFLP. We know there is a network of former Nazi Party Officers manipulating Al Fatah cells, as well as others like DFLP, and certain Soviet-based anti-Semitic organizations. However, it is more difficult for these groups to gain traction in the Soviet Union as the USSR would prefer to support groups like Black September from a distance and not become directly involved. Roland seeks to become directly involved, which is why he engaged the DFLP."

"This just keeps getting better and better."

"We had a near miss with him in Argentina, just last year," Saul said. "However, we are not certain that your Rollo is our Roland."

Ronald shot Saul a dirty look.

"Only one way to find out," Ronald said and reaching into his jacket pocket he retrieved a black-and-white photo and laid it on the table in front of Will. It was Rollo, much younger, but it was him.

"That's him."

"Case closed. You're out," Ronald said, taking the photo and putting it back in his pocket. "SFPD's going to handle this, Saul."

"You know we cannot do it that way," Saul argued. "You will not be able to follow the international trail."

"I'll run it up to the CIA."

"Who will have no 'in' with the group."

"Then I will just bust this fucking neo-Nazi and haul his ass in. Case closed. Interpol has a beef with him and the Reds want his ass too, so as far as I'm concerned, they can pull an Abraham and each have half."

"And then the group breaks away and you have another bombed synagogue or worse!" Saul snapped. "This is bigger than you and it's bigger than him!"

Ronald hesitated for a moment, and the older man continued.

"You know that I am right," Saul said evenly. "There are other groups, not just this one."

"What other groups?" Will asked. The two men turned to look at him.

"Organizations like Al Fatah and the DFLP set these groups up like bombs on a timer," Ronald began. "They put them together so that each group can continue to function if one gets taken down. Most likely Roland was responsible for putting this group together several months ago, maybe by writing letters via an ad placed in a magazine or newspaper."

"They've definitely met before," Will interrupted.

"Really?" Ronald seemed surprised.

"Yeah, they knew each other by sight." Will thought about it for a moment. It was obvious

Saul and Ronald knew a lot more about this guy than he did, but all the same Will understood that they were missing a piece to the puzzle that was fairly important. "There's something else. I don't think he'll be able to dispose of this group that easily."

"What makes you say that?" Ronald asked.

"Because he's in love with my girlfriend."

Ronald stared at Will hard. In the blink of an eye, the young man had suddenly become indispensable.

"You're sure about this?" Saul asked.

"I'm sure," Will replied. He had picked up on it when Mary chastised Rollo in Mexico and the Russian instantly became quiet.

"Fine," Ronald said. "It looks like you're the man."

CHAPTER 12

Will Hessler felt cold, alone, and out on a ledge with nothing to hold on to. He sat with Mary, Rollo, Maxwell and Randall in a small Italian restaurant in San Francisco's North Beach neighborhood. Rollo was working on a giant plate of spaghetti while the others occupied themselves with other assorted dishes. Will's ravioli sat in front of him only half-eaten. He kept telling himself that he needed to pull it together, to not give Rollo or the others any reason to be suspicious of him.

"I didn't know who you were, out in the desert," Rollo said, talking with his mouth half-full of pasta. "If I had known who you were, who your mother and grandfather were, I never would have pulled that shit. In my book, you are beyond suspicion."

If Will hadn't been so nervous, he probably would have burst out laughing. Mary held his hand beneath the table, and the touch of her skin made his crawl.

"There's no way you could have known," Will said. "It was pretty random."

"Agreed," Rollo replied in a manner bordering on being a command. "It's good for us though, good for the organization to have you on board. Your experience is invaluable."

Will took a pause, not wanting to seem like he was pumping Rollo for information. If he could just end the whole thing that night over dinner, it would be all the better.

"Invaluable for what?" Will asked.

Rollo looked at him squarely and stopped chewing.

"What do you know about history, Will?"

"Not much I guess," Will answered. It was true, he didn't know as much as he thought he should, unless Rollo wanted to hear the entire history of the Jewish people, which Will felt was highly unlikely.

"Are you familiar with the Armenian genocide?"

"I've heard of it."

"That's a good example of a people who saw the threat coming and did nothing. I see the threat," Rollo said, poking his thumb in his chest. "I see these people for what they are. I don't have a problem with the struggle, with fighting for something. If we were invaded by a foreign power tomorrow, I would be proud to fight for my country, to die for it if need be. But to wake up tomorrow in a country where Jews and niggers control the lives of white men and realize I could have done something to prevent it? I would be ashamed to fight that war, ashamed of myself."

Will did know about the Armenian Genocide. He knew about it because his grandfather had spoken of it as a good working model for what the Nazis had done during World War II. It struck Will as blackly ironic that Rollo was using as an example of his struggle, an incident that so closely mirrored the horror wrought by a group that thought the same way he did.

Will watched Rollo eat his pasta, watched the gears turn inside the man's head, and watched him become more and more dangerous as the minutes ticked by. Like those fueled by fear, a machine that runs on hatred never rests.

Will began to develop an almost violent reaction to Mary Gauss. Previously he had thought that dealing with Rollo or even Maxwell and Randall would be the most difficult part, but that turned out to be quite easy as he had no personal connection to them. They were just animals. The hardest part was spending time with Mary. Will began vomiting when he had to touch her for prolonged periods of time. He told her that he had some sort of stomach flu, but soon enough just learned to cover it up.

A doctor told him he was developing an ulcer, most likely induced by stress and by the repeated vomiting. Will chewed antacids incessantly and said they were mints. Later he would find out he came dangerously close to developing aluminum poisoning from it. All of the sharks he was swimming with, and he was nearly taken out by antacids.

More and more Will was thinking of

Susanne Bonafide, and how if he ever got out of this mess, he would try to do right by her.

Will knew that Rollo had a flat in the Richmond and was keeping the crate there, or at the very least nearby. Aside from wanting to keep people away due to his illegal activities, Rollo was a naturally solitary person, so Will couldn't just invite himself over to drink some beers and watch the game. He wracked his brain trying to think of a way to gain access to Rollo's apartment but came up empty every time.

It felt like a dead end. This had always been a possibility, that he might just hit a wall and there would be nothing more to do. They would have to shut the operation down. At this same time, Will began having nightmares about being at the synagogue after his mother had blown it up. Seeing the bodies, the destruction and carnage. He knew that he would do anything he had to in order to stop that from happening again.

Anything.

"I know a way to get close to Rollo."

Ronald and Will walked down Embarcadero in the early morning drinking coffee and watching people running and commuting to work. It occurred to Will that the concept of "working hours" was not something that really applied to the two of them. They were just two cogs in a greater machine tumbling through life with a single-minded purpose.

"How?"

"Mary Gauss. She could have his full confidence inside of a day."

Ronald stopped and looked at Will.

"And how would you propose we pull that one off? Last I heard she was pretty committed to the cause, and to you."

"I think she's more committed to not going to prison."

Ronald shook his head.

"That's a risky play, Will. Got anything we can nail her on?"

"I'm sure we can come up with something."

"This just keeps getting further and further out there, Will. No matter what Saul thinks, he may have opened this can of worms, but SFPD will be the ones to close it. He may not think he has to play by the rules, but for something like this we have to. You and I both know how easily a case can be thrown out of court if it's put together the wrong way."

"You have an idea of what the right way looks like?"

"Something to get her on? You're a better judge than me, Will. What's something illegal she might take the bait on?"

Will thought about it for a moment. Mary would probably do just about anything to support the cause, but what was something he could lead her to?

"I'll have to think about it."

"Just keep it simple. When stuff like this gets too complicated that's when it starts falling apart."

Amidst the noise of everything that was happening, Will and Susanne had developed something of a truce. One could even say it was a friendship. Once a week they would meet to catch a movie or have dinner together. They would talk about old times and exchange furtive glances. Will knew that she was still desperately in love with him, and his feelings for her grew stronger every day, but the timing wasn't right. In the shadow of what Will had discovered Mary Gauss to be, Susanne shone stronger than ever before.

They tried to make small talk, but it was always just their way of dancing around the ghost of what they used to be.

"Will, I'm worried about these people you're hanging out with."

Will almost dropped his fork.

"What people?"

"That girl and those guys." Susanne looked self-conscious, as if she were afraid he was going to think she was spying on him. "I'm not spying on you, Will. At least not—not in a bad way. My friend Gina, she takes some classes over at City College, she's seen you with them. She says they're..."

Will waited for her to finish, but she didn't.

"They're what?" he asked.

"I'm not sure, Will, but... Gina said she heard that Mary girl say something about..." Will could tell Susanne didn't want to repeat what she had heard. "She said something about Jews. Something not complimentary."

Will looked down at his hands to avoid her eyes. He thought about the operation and telling Susanne the truth. He couldn't stand the thought of Susanne thinking that he was of a like mind with Mary, Randall, and Max. She didn't even have knowledge of Rollo yet, and Will couldn't imagine how that would go over. It wouldn't so much be the anti-Semitism as the idea of him hanging around with someone like him. Mary, Randall, and Maxwell could all clean themselves up and fit in with polite society, but not so with Federov. One look at him and you knew he wasn't someone you should turn your back on.

"Look, Will, if you're feeling those same things I want you to be honest with me about it. I won't judge you."

"No," he cut her off. "I don't feel that way."

"Then I don't understand why you would be friends with them."

Will tapped his fingers on the table nervously.

"I'm not like them, Susanne, I don't feel those things. There's more going on than you know."

"So tell me."

He did. Will told her everything. More than just people and places, he also communicated the feelings and emotions he was experiencing. It was all the equivalent of being in the back seat of a car perpetually spinning out of control, the wheel always just out of his reach.

Susanne took Will's hands in hers.

"Tonight you'll stay with me, and in the morning, I want you to talk to my father."

"Why?"

"I want you to talk to Dad, because he is not necessarily what he seems, and he may be able to help."

Nothing surprised Will Hessler anymore, so he just accepted it.

"And you want me to stay with you?"

"Because sometimes I think you forget how important it is to just have someone hold you in the night and remind you that it's all going to be okay."

In the morning, Susanne brought Will to a semi-awake state with a pot of coffee and some eggs and bacon. It was if he had not experienced a good night's sleep in a thousand years.

Will had no idea what to expect from this meeting with Susanne's father. Apparently

Carl Bonafide had started working for the CIA after Vietnam, but Will did not know how that connected to what he was mixed up in, unless Susanne just figured there should be some vague connection between the two of them. However, Will knew Susanne better than that and figured she had something more substantial cooking in that brain of hers.

He was correct.

Will talked to Carl Bonafide for over an hour, and told him absolutely everything that had happened. It did feel as if he was violating some vow of secrecy, but Ronald and Saul had never said anything about not discussing what was going on outside of the group of people directly involved. Perhaps it was assumed, but Will didn't care.

Susanne thought that her father was working as an analyst for the Central Intelligence Agency, but Will suspected this was not the case. She knew he had some connection with the tracking of Nazi war criminals and had recently taken business trips to the Middle East, which was why she thought he might be able to give Will some advice. It turned out he would provide more than just advice.

"Jesus Christ, Will, you are hip deep in a world of shit."

"Yes, Sir," Will responded.

Carl stood up from behind his desk and walked across the room to one of the shelves in his study. He retrieved a book and opening it pulled out a photo that was between some pages and handed it to Will.

"That's Jurgen Steiner. Two weeks ago, I snuck him across the border from Egypt to Israel where he was tried and executed. He was an SS Commander during the war, identified by several former Dachau inmates as having committed atrocities, primarily against women and children. I would have preferred to save the time and hassle and just shoot him in the desert, but the Jews have become real sticklers for due process. At least when it's relatively convenient."

Will looked at the photo, and the cold eyes staring back at him.

Carl pointed at an Arab man standing beside Steiner in the photograph.

"That's Said Al Assan, a known DFLP

faction leader. Democratic Front for the Liberation of Palestine."

"I don't mean to be rude Sir, but why are you telling me this?"

Carl sat on the edge of his desk and looked down at Will.

"As I said, Will, you're up to your hips in this shit. I think you deserve to know what kind of shit it is."

"What kind of shit is it?"

"Jurgen was helping DFLP organize something, but we don't know what. We figure Steiner was here to meet Said and get him set up. It's a little trickier than he's accustomed to because he's so far from his traditional operating base."

"So, you targeted Steiner specifically because of that? Not just because he's a war criminal?"

"Don't get me wrong, Will, we fully support the efforts of Israel and independents like Wiesenthal who are tracking down these bastards, but it is not the job of the United States and specifically the CIA to track down Nazi war criminals. We just want to make sure we thoroughly break the back of this alliance before it gets any traction. If a terror group like DFLP manages to pull off an attack here, things could quickly get out of hand."

"Do you think Saul knows about this?"

"I think Inspector Stein is in the dark, but I guarantee you Saul knows exactly what is going on. He's just giving you the pieces of the puzzle he thinks you need to know to get the job done. I don't play that way."

"How do you play?"

"We knew about Federov. We've been tracking him since he crossed paths with Steiner ten years ago, but we lost him a year ago in South America. Jurgen managed to get himself thrown in a Soviet prison in sixty-seven trying to buy weapons to start an insurrection in West Germany. The Soviets didn't know who they had, so he was just doing his time when he met Federov and saw an eager disciple. Jurgen was a vicious fighter in his day, but by the time he hit Kolyma Prison he was older and needed protection. Plus, Soviets in general don't take kindly to former German soldiers. Federov was only twenty, but he had already developed a singular talent for killing. It didn't take much for Jurgen to mold Federov. That boy never knew a home or a father figure before Jurgen. For two years, they worked together on the inside trying to get something going in West Germany. You may not be aware of it, but there was a resistance in Germany after the war. Nazi holdouts were fighting the occupation forces. By the time Jurgen and Federov started working together, the insurrection had long since died out. Still, Jurgen was convinced he could light the flame again and build a reunited Germany—reunified under a fourth Reich. But he also knew that with every passing day the chances of pulling it off became slimmer.

"In sixty-nine, there was a full-scale riot at Kolyma, and unfortunately that's where the trail went cold until Federov resurfaced two years later, and Jurgen reappeared in Egypt two months ago."

"Where was Jurgen?" Will asked.

"No one knows. That's what bothered me about it. Jurgen wasn't spending his time collecting stamps after Kolyma. He was still working for the cause. I have no proof, but I know. So my problem is that for six years this guy is a ghost, in full operations mode and always able to escape detection. Then suddenly a CIA informant spots him at a fruit stand in Alexandria? I don't buy it, I never did, but I ran the pick up anyway."

"Sir, if he's dead I don't understand."

"He's not dead. I don't think the Israelis ever executed him."

"Why?"

"I have a couple theories," Carl replied. "It's unlikely, but possible that officials were bribed and documents including the death certificate were forged. More likely is that the Mossad had Jurgen released under the pretense that he was "escaping" so that they could find out what he had been up to, and try to track the rest of his conspirators. That's Saul's connection. He's trying to get all the players. The problem is that Jurgen is not just another Nazi war criminal that needs to get picked up. He's a major power broker in the new resistance with big-time connections."

"Wait a minute. How do you know Jurgen is still alive?"

Carl pointed to the black-and-white picture of Jurgen that was now sitting on his desk.

"Because that was taken three days ago by airport security at SFO. It was totally random that the head of airport security is a Nazi history fanatic and recognized Jurgen. He kept it to himself and forwarded the photo to the FBI. Agent Halliwell in the SF branch office knew I had supposedly delivered Jurgen into the hands of his executioners and called me. That's a little something we call luck, Will. Right now, as far as we know, the information loop remains closed and only a handful of people know that Jurgen is still alive. Way I figure it, Jurgen was meeting Said at the airport, and then he took the next plane out."

"Christ!" Will spat and stood up. "I didn't want any of this. I was willing to help—happy to help when it was just some kids doing who knows what, but now this?"

"You're sort of a glass half empty kind of guy, aren't you?"

"Live my life Mister Bonafide and tell me I shouldn't see things that way."

With no change of expression, Carl tapped his prosthetic leg against the desk.

"You haven't cornered the market on loss, Will. Your stock is up, but there's always plenty to go around. The decisions you make now are what separate you from all those other people out there that don't believe in anything greater than themselves. You can walk away if you want, but you'll be leaving a trail of dead bodies behind you."

"So what do I do?" Will asked, feeling exasperated.

"Inspector Stein is a good man. Just follow his lead and I'll be working on your behalf behind the scenes.

"What about Saul?"

Carl paused for a moment, and it was obvious that he was carefully framing what he was about to say.

"Saul Greenbaum is a legend within the Mossad, and really the entire intelligence community. I will tell you though, part of the reason he built that reputation is that he doesn't hesitate to make sacrifices if it will get the job done."

"Like the human kind?"

Carl held up his hands.

"I didn't say that, but it's not far from the truth. Just watch yourself with him."

CHAPTER 13

After much consideration on the subject of how to entrap Mary Gauss, Will had come up with a solution that seemed foolproof.

Mary had a penchant for historical items from the Third Reich. Her grandfather had started her on collecting, and she owned a respectable assortment of twisted antiquities. One item in particular that Will knew she had a morbid fascination with was Zyklon B, an insecticide used to produce the gas that killed Jews in the death camps.

"Are you kidding me?" The look in her eyes bordered on madness. "It's sealed?"

That had actually been quite a trick. Saul managed to come through in procuring a sealed container of Zyklon B, and Will did not really want to know where he found it.

"Yeah, they found it at a warehouse in a crate with some other stuff secured during the clearing out of Auschwitz. It's even stamped with the camp name in German."

"That's incredible. And he only wants twenty dollars?"

"I don't think he knows what it is. He said he just bought the stuff in a government lot auction. Funniest part is he's Jewish."

Mary burst out laughing and Will had to turn away sharply to hide the fact that he was about to vomit yet again.

"We should go get it now!" Mary snapped. "Before someone else does. Do you have any idea how much that canister is worth? To a collector, I mean. It's priceless."

Will looked at his watch.

"Okay, let's go."

"You already set it up?"

Will smiled, a mask to cover his inner disdain for every breath she took, and his desire to strangle each one out of her.

"Of course. I knew you would want it. He's going to meet us in a half hour."

Mary threw her arms around him and buried her face in his neck. Will could feel her shark's smile against his flesh. Happiness brought about by an artifact of the death of millions.

"Will," she whispered. "I think I'm falling in love with you."

After Mary Gauss professed her love for him, Will had not said anything in return. Perhaps she took his silence as agreement. He knew that in many ways Mary Gauss was going to be destroyed by the planned betrayal, and admitted to himself that he took a sort of twisted pleasure in knowing how it was going to hurt her. Mary Gauss was Will Hessler's smiling black plague, a creature that caused him pain and general dissatisfaction at every turn. She deserved whatever happened to her.

In too many ways, Mary was a mirror of Diane Hessler. She had an infinite capacity for sweetness and kindness, but only if you were the correct color. She had an equally bottomless well of anger and hatred that stemmed from who only knew where, and it was this stagnant well from which she drew her strength.

Inspector Ronald Stein would pose as the seller of illegal goods, and in this role he met the two at his door. Without much in the way of conversation Ronald led them into the kitchen. A plain cardboard box sat on the otherwise empty table.

"You sure you want to buy this stuff?"

Mary fancied herself to be a shrewd customer, so she attempted to hide her enthusiasm.

"Of course, it's what I came here for."

"All right, but if someone asks you where you got it, you don't know me, understand? I mean, I'm not sure why you would even want this thing, but I get the feeling I'm not supposed to have it."

"I won't rat you out," Mary assured him. "It's just going to go into storage with the rest of my stuff."

Will looked around the house as Ronald and Mary talked. He had never been this close to Inspector Stein's personal life, and never really thought about him having one. Now Will saw photos of him on the wall with what could only be his wife or girlfriend. Will figured most likely a girlfriend, as the house was in disarray, and it did not look like a woman lived there. Dishes were piled up in the sink; trash had overflowed from the garbage can and littered the floor.

Picking up the cardboard box, Ronald opened it and carefully removed an aluminum canister, which he then handed to Mary. Mary's eyes were wide with horrific joy as she rotated the canister in her hands, reading the German script on the label.

"Twenty dollars, right?" Mary asked, raising an eyebrow.

Ronald nodded his agreement.

Mary carefully set the canister back in the box and closed the lid. Reaching into her pocket, she retrieved a twenty-dollar bill and handed it to Inspector Stein.

Ronald looked at the twenty for a moment and then pulled out the small black wallet with his badge in it and dropped it open on the table. Will noticed that the ID card normally held in the upper half was gone but did not think much of it.

"Now sit down you little psychopath."

. . .

Mary sat quietly as Inspector Stein laid it all out for her, and told her that if she did not cooperate, she would be indicted on a charge of attempting to purchase a chemical weapon and would most likely never feel sunlight on her skin again.

They had considered trying to make it look like Will had nothing to do with the deception to maintain his cover with Mary, but it would have made things much more difficult. They needed her to feel like she could work freely around him.

Mary looked scared, so scared that she was sweating. Will also sensed a rage building beneath the surface. Her green eyes twitched as she listened to him tell her how she was going to collect information for them and use Rollo's affections for her to find out what was in the crate.

Mary did not nod or say a word to confirm that she understood, and it wasn't really necessary. There was no way she was not acutely aware of everything that was happening to her, everything that was being done to her.

. . .

Neither Mary nor Will spoke as they drove back to the Lower Haight part of town. Mary just stared out the window.

Will pulled up outside of her apartment building and cut the engine on the DeSoto. Mary seemed in a daze, possibly even unaware that they had arrived at her home. He leaned in a little and quietly said, "Mary."

It was as if he had sent an electric shock through her. Her eyes bored into him for a moment and then she relented, most likely because she knew immediate rage would profit her nothing. Will would have preferred it if she had just rammed his head through the driver's side window right then and there and been done with it. Mary, however, had other ideas.

"Will." There was a pause where she must have been appreciating the palpable tension in the air between them, tight as a tripwire. "You're going to pay for what you did to me."

The look on Mary's face was not anger, or hatred, or even disappointment. It almost seemed to be more along the lines of pity and regret.

. . .

"I don't know if this was such a great idea. She's really pissed."

"It was the only card we had to play, Will." Inspector Stein's voice was calm and steady over the phone. "If she wants to stay out of jail, she'll work with us."

"And what if she doesn't care? What if her desire to get back at me is stronger than anything else?"

"Then I guess you're screwed." Ronald paused. "I'm sorry, that was a bad joke. This is your life we're messing with here. I just really think Mary will toe the line. I've been doing this a while, I've learned to read people. I think we're good."

"Have you heard anything from Saul?"

"No... Saul's back in Israel."

Will almost dropped the phone.

"He's what?"

"Will, I know this is bad timing, but Saul is managing several operations at any given time. He can't be hands on with this, as much as he might like to. That's why I'm staying as involved as I am." Ronald quickly added, "And of course because I don't want to see you get hurt."

"I know, I understand. I have to go."

Will hung up the phone and stared at it. He felt deceitful for not telling Ronald about working with Carl Bonafide. No one was supposed to know Carl was as deep in with the CIA as he was, so it wasn't really an option either way.

It was all getting so convoluted that Will was losing track of who he even was. He considered that the concept of feeling as if he were deceiving Ronald was a silly one since he was deceiving nearly everyone he knew in one way or another.

The phone rang, and Will nearly jumped out of his skin. He snatched up the receiver.

"Hello?"

"Will, I need you to meet me. Now."

It was Rollo on the other end of the line; sounding very serious.

"About what? I'm kind of busy, Rollo."

"It has come to my attention that we have a traitor among us."

Will's breath caught in his throat.

"Who?"

"Just meet me in the park in an hour, by the windmill." Rollo paused. "Bring a shovel."

As soon as Rollo hung up, Will called Inspector Stein and told him what had just transpired. Ronald said he would be in the park, well away from the meeting to keep an eye on things. Despite this reassurance, Will felt like the proverbial worm on the hook, dangling out there all by himself.

It was twilight by the time he reached the part of the park Rollo had wanted to meet at. The formidable looking Russian stood in the grass near the windmill and Will could see Maxwell and Mary standing with him. Mary looked at Will, and he could see the anger seething behind her eyes. Maybe Inspector Stein was wrong, and her desire to be free was not stronger than her desire to make him pay.

"Where's your shovel?" Rollo asked.

"I don't own a shovel, Rollo. Why would I have a shovel?"

Rollo tossed Will a shovel and walked toward the tree line with Mary, Maxwell, and him following.

"I trust you motherfuckers about as far as I can throw you," Rollo said, seemingly talking to no one in particular. "So, I wasn't about to trust you with the real location of the crate."

"Wait a minute." Will stopped. "What was in the other crate?"

Rollo looked over his shoulder. He wasn't looking at Will, but into him.

"A dead body. Any more questions Curious Yellow Monkey?"

It seemed that Rollo was trying to reference Curious George, and Will found it very odd that he felt the need to compare him to a cartoon monkey, and also that a Soviet knew who Curious George was.

"No."

The four of them stopped in a clearing beneath a tree, and began the work of digging. After quite a while, Will felt his shovel hit wood, and knew that it must be the crate they were digging for. He was tempted to "accidentally" drive his shovel through the top in hopes of discovering what was locked inside but decided against this tactic as it would be too obvious. Even if Rollo bought the ruse, the man would not want to leave any room for error and would most likely execute Will on the spot.

Whatever was in the crate it was packed

tight, and despite the weight it was fairly easy to lift out of the ground. No explanation of what they were doing was given as Rollo directed them to hoist the crate into the trunk of his car.

Rollo slammed the lid shut and turned to the three of them.

"This is the time for you to get out. If you have any doubts about what we're doing, if you think this is some fucking summer camp that you can leave any time you want, now is the time to say so. In two minutes, you're not going to have that choice anymore."

Will looked at Mary and Maxwell, and saw that they were looking at him.

"I don't want out," Mary said, staring directly at Will. "I'm committed to the cause."

"So am I," Maxwell agreed.

"I'm in," Will said.

"Good."

Rollo walked to the passenger side rear door of his vehicle and opened it. He grabbed something and roughly yanked it out of the car and onto the ground.

It was Randall's body, with a clean bullet hole between the eyes. Will could tell that the man had been badly beaten before he was shot. This was meant to be a warning.

"If you try to walk on me, you share his fate. We're seeing this thing through to the finish, and when it's over the whole world will hear our message."

They buried Randall in the park with no markings to let the world know where he lay. The four sat in silence as they drove back to Rollo's place in the Sunset. He parked outside the small in-law house and the four manhandled the crate from the trunk of the car and into Rollo's place.

Rollo's house was just like the apartment he had moved there from. Virtually no furnishings, nothing on the walls, nothing to indicate that a real human being with likes or dislikes lived there, someone with friends and family. There was, however, every indication that a Rollo lived there.

They set the crate down on the living room floor in the semi-darkness. Rollo flicked the lights on and Will almost fell over at the sight of the stranger sitting in a chair in the corner.

For the first time in an instance not associated with Mary, Will saw Rollo smile.

"Hello, my friend," the man said, speaking with an Arabic accent. He stood up and shook Rollo's hand, and Will saw something significant. He had previously noticed that Rollo had a series of numbers and letters tattooed on his right forearm. This man had them as well, and Will memorized the series.

"It is good to see you," Rollo replied. They both turned and looked at the others in the room. "These are my associates."

The man walked up to each of them and shook their hands.

"My name is Said Al Assan. I am grateful for your assistance. We all are."

Said turned to Rollo and rattled off something in Arabic. Rollo laughed and replied also in Arabic, though not without some effort.

Will memorized both.

Said Al Assan was now in play.

"Do they know they are to be martyred?"

Carl dropped the paper onto his desk and looked at Will. Carl Bonafide did not speak

Arabic himself, so he had sent out what Will memorized to a translator, and the translator returned those eight words.

"We're supposed to die?"

"Apparently, and those numbers you memorized really explain a lot about how Said, Rollo, and Jurgen are linked. Said was in Kolyma Prison with Rollo and Jurgen, and more recently he was involved in the planning of the Ma'alot Massacre."

"I'm not familiar with it."

"Gunmen in northern Israel took control of a high school. They killed 26, wounded over 60. In general, Fatah and the terror organizations under its umbrella had a big streak this year, pulled off a lot of attacks. General wisdom in the intel community is that this is the establishment of a trend, and it's just going to get worse."

"For what reason?"

"I think they're bringing the kettle to a boil, Will. I think there's something big on the horizon. You don't keep attacking your enemy with fleabites when you have the ability to chop his head off. Al Fatah believes we're the ones behind Israel, and they're correct in that thinking. In line with that logic it would make sense that any wound visited upon us will be visited upon Israel tenfold."

"And you think they're behind what Rollo and Said are doing?"

"It's possible, but the DFLP are pretty militant about not going outside their borders to launch attacks, unless I'm right and they want to punish Israel by hitting us. Wound the Americans and maybe they'll stop supporting the Jews, that type of thing. It's possible they were inspired by Munich to extend their fiery sword beyond the borders of Israel/Palestine and go for the big win. Or it could be something as silly as a pissing contest between them and Black September for street cred."

"Can't you just arrest these guys or something? Isn't there enough?"

Carl rubbed his hands together and looked troubled.

"Will, you have to believe one of my prime motivations is to get you out of this business as soon as humanly possible, but I also think there is more to this than what we're seeing right now. All parties agree that the crate is most likely full of explosives. Our problem is that we don't know where those explosives came from, or even if that's the only crate. It doesn't do us any good to shut down this cell if two weeks later the L Train gets bombed in Chicago."

"I understand, and I'm committed to seeing this thing through, I just need to know what to do."

"We have to get inside that crate, which will be a little more difficult now that Al Assan is in the picture. Any security holes Rollo may have left open Said definitely closed. I'm thinking the explosives are something high grade like C-4. If it is C-4, then it will be tagged with an originator code. If we get that code, we can find out where the hell it came from and close that source up. They may have stripped it, but I doubt it. Stripping it would mean acknowledging the possibility they could be infiltrated, and I don't think Said or Rollo's egos will allow for that. Our secondary objective is to find out where the hell Jurgen is. This guy just dropped off the map."

"You have no idea where he is?"

Will could tell that Carl Bonafide was bothered by this. The CIA agent liked to have control over every situation, and in this instance, he was lacking that control.

"He could be in my bathroom and I wouldn't know it." Leaning over, Carl pulled open a desk drawer and retrieved a stack of papers. After rifling through them he handed one to Will. It was a class registration sheet for City College. The class was beginning Arabic.

"What's this?" Will asked.

"Now that this new element has been introduced, i.e. Said Al Assan, I think it would be a good idea if you picked up Arabic."

"Picked up Arabic?" Will asked. Carl made it sound so easy, like learning a new trick on your bicycle.

"I think you'll be surprised by how easily it comes to you, Will. I think you have a talent for languages. You already speak fluent German, Hebrew and Spanish. If it were up to me, I'd sock you into one of the accelerated programs down at the Defense Language Institute in Monterey, but until then this will have to do. If you find it too easy, I'll get you bumped into the next level."

"Mr. Bonafide, I'm not trying to sound

ungrateful, but I thought the idea was to get me out of this, not sink me in deeper?"

"Will, I wouldn't do this if I didn't think it might very likely save your life someday soon. Knowing what Said is saying and being able to translate on the fly will help you quickly make informed decisions and be more efficient."

Will looked at the sheet of paper in his hand. He knew that Carl was right.

"Okay," Will said. "I can do this."

All that Will had to do was get past Rollo and Said to read the tags on the explosives, find a former Nazi master of counter intelligence, and learn Arabic—all while keeping tabs on the possibly explosive element of Mary Gauss.

"I see no problem with any of this," Ronald said.

Ronald Stein looked like he had been hit by a truck as he sat across from Will in the Church Street diner, chain smoking and going over papers chronicling different aspects of the investigation.

"I'm not worried," Will replied. "For once. It actually seems like all of this is going to work out. I feel like there's an actual plan to follow, I'm not just winging it. We're supposed to meet tonight to talk about the 'first phase'. That's what Rollo calls it."

"Maybe he'll do us a favor and bust open that crate. You can memorize the tag numbers and be done with it."

"What about Said?"

"I'll take care of Said."

"How so?" Will asked.

"Let me worry about that. It's better if you don't know. Suffice it to say, you take care of those tag numbers, I'll take care of the Arab."

Something about the way Ronald said this made Will very uncomfortable. Ronald was one of the few people he trusted implicitly, and he was also one of the only people who had been there for him from the very beginning, seemingly never asking for anything in return. Despite this, Will's cynical nature meant that he could not help but wonder when the bill for services rendered would come due.

"I'm going to start running surveillance on Rollo's place during your meetings. If you get the tag numbers, I want you to step outside to smoke a cigarette, stretch your arms out, and then drop the cigarette to the ground and go back inside."

"And then what?"

"And then this will be over."

"I don't like it."

"He's taken me this far."

Will could hear the hesitancy in Carl Bonafide's voice on the other end of the phone.

"Have you ever known Ronald to do anything crazy? Do you think he's unstable?"

"He's seemed a little odd lately, but to be honest Ronald is about the most stable person I've ever met."

"I'm going to do a little checking, Will. I don't think this is an SFPD-sanctioned investigation he's conducting. If it isn't, I want to know what Inspector Stein's motivation is."

That night Will went to his first Arabic class out at City College. Carl Bonafide had been correct. It was scary how fast he picked it up. He even managed to pull apart and translate the things the teacher would say when she was showing off. It was something about figuring out the basics—body language, facial expressions, etc. Once he had those down, everything else fell into place.

Will had not spoken with Susanne much, partially because he had to maintain his identity as Mary Gauss's boyfriend and going out with Susanne was not conducive to pulling that off. All it would take was Maxwell or Rollo seeing the two of them together to make things much more difficult. Will returned home that night to find Mary sitting on the floor reading a book. She was apparently intent on maintaining the illusion as well.

Will said nothing to her, and she returned the favor as he went about preparing himself a meal and mentally going over his schedule for the next day.

"Rollo called." Will almost jumped out of his skin when she spoke. "He wants us to go to his place tonight to get further instructions."

"After I get something to eat, we'll head over there."

"Why do you hate me, Will?"

Will looked down at her.

"I don't hate you, Mary. We're both just caught in the middle of this thing."

"You turned me over to that fucking Jew cop, Will!" Mary snapped. "You helped him entrap me, goddammit!"

"You did this to yourself! You're just like my mother, always trying to blame someone else for your actions!"

"Fuck you, Will! I would be proud to be like your mother! You're nothing but a goddamn disappointment to her, and if I had known how different you are from Diane, I would have sooner set you on fire than speak to you!"

Will studied Mary Gauss for a moment. She had the same maniacal glare in her eyes that his mother always had.

"Thank you."

"For what?" Mary spat in disgust.

"I was starting to feel sorry for you."

"Fuck you and your pity."

Will paused for a moment, unsure if he should say what was on his mind.

"They're planning on killing all of us," he said without looking at her. "That is what Said was saying when he spoke to Rollo, after he shook our hands. He said we are to be martyred."

"Jewish lies."

"Believe what you want. When we go over there tonight, you're going to get Rollo alone with you in another room. I don't care what you have to do. I'll get into that crate, and we'll be done with this. I can go back to my life, and you can go back to...whatever it is you do."

Mary said nothing, and her silence was deafening.

They arrived at Rollo's house late, near midnight. No one else was there, and the place was dead silent as he brought Will and Mary into the living room. The ever-present crate sat on two planks suspended by a set of cinderblocks. There was no lock on it, nothing. It almost seemed too inviting, too easy.

Looking around, Will saw a Muni transit map tacked to the wall with different points marked on it, mostly along the Market Street corridor. Alongside of it was a map of another city, also with points marked along a main route. The map had been drawn by hand with intricate detail, but nothing was named, no streets, nothing. Will did his best to memorize the features in hopes of later figuring out where it was. A third map was of the city of Hamburg, in Germany.

Mary took Rollo to the side and began speaking with him. Will noticed she had placed her hand on Rollo's shoulder in a familiar way. Rollo kept looking at him as if something suspicious were going on.

"Don't touch anything," Rollo said, and a moment later he went into the next room with Mary.

Will did not hesitate. He moved quickly and quietly across the room and checked around the crate lid for anything Rollo or Said might have left to indicate that someone had tampered with it. Perhaps a piece of string or tape connecting the lid to the box. Will kept glancing at the door, waiting for Rollo to walk in on him and deliver him into the next world.

Will reached out to lift the lid, and then watched the crate rush away from him, quickly realizing that he was flying backward, and that someone had yanked him away by the collar. Will looked up from the floor to see Carl

Bonafide standing over him in Rollo's apartment.

"Leave it closed," he whispered, and before Will could think to say anything, Carl walked back out the open door and was gone.

Will stood up a moment before Rollo walked back into the room with Mary and tried not to look nervous.

"An hour before you were at Rollo's house about to open that crate, an identical crate was opened in Hamburg, Germany. Thirteen people were killed in the blast."

"Jesus Christ. You mean that crate I was about to open..."

"Would have vaporized you. I'm sorry, Will; I didn't think they would rig the crate to explode because whatever is in there is so damn valuable to them. I was wrong."

Will was angry, but he also couldn't get mad at Carl. He knew the man was doing everything he could for him, and no one could be right every time. All the same, Will started sweating just thinking about how close he had come to death.

"Was it explosives in the crate?"

"They don't know. It was just dumb luck that they even found out about it. A cop in a bar overheard the landlord talking about having rented an apartment to a bunch of Arabs and that they were up at all hours, lots of activity going on. Ever since Munich the Germans have been chomping at the bit for a chance to break in their counter-terror unit, GSG-9. Well, they got their chance. They figure the crate was packed with a security layer of explosives, but that layer was only there to protect something else inside."

"What?"

Carl shrugged.

"We don't know. What we do know now is that we're dealing with a multi-cell event. This isn't just about blowing up a synagogue in San Francisco, or even two synagogues. They're trying to do something that will get them recognized. Sometime tonight or tomorrow Rollo and Said will find out about the Hamburg blast, and they'll want to accelerate their timetable."

Will remembered the maps.

"There were three maps on the wall. One was of Hamburg, one of San Francisco, and another one I didn't recognize. It was hand drawn, no street names, no nothing."

"Do you think if I gave you a map book you could find it?"

"I don't think that will be necessary."

"Why?"

"Because it's on the wall behind you."

Looking over his shoulder Carl's eyes settled on the framed city map of Tel Aviv, Israel.

"I feel like I'm going to break."

Will sat on Susanne's bed, and she sat beside him holding his hand.

"Will, is my father trying to make you do something you don't want to do?"

"No, he's not. In the beginning I was just doing it because it had to be done, but now things are different."

"What?"

He looked at her.

"I'm starting to like it. Is that weird?"

"I just don't understand how something that is so hard on you could be something you like?"

"I'm good at it. I'm picking things up quickly."

"What about your painting?"

Will shook his head.

"I don't know. I don't know what to think about anything anymore."

Without saying anything else he curled up on the bed and lay his head in her lap.

In the morning, Will sat at the breakfast table in the Bonafide household eating his first full-fledged meal in weeks. Sunshine came in through the bay windows and helped make him feel like a human being again.

More and more his inability to be with Susanne was causing him pain. When it would have been easy, he turned her away, and now that it was next to impossible, he could not bear to be away from her.

"Good morning."

Will looked up to see Carl walking into the kitchen.

"Good morning," Will replied.

"Inspector Stein is no longer employed by

or affiliated with the San Francisco Police Department."

Will almost dropped his toast.

"What?"

"Ronald was put on administrative leave three months ago pending a psychiatric evaluation. He chose not to pursue it and put in his letter of resignation."

There had been no I.D. card next to Ronald's badge. The pieces fell into place all at once.

"Jesus Christ. He doesn't care about making a case; he just wants to get all of them."

"What?" Carl asked.

"Ronald had a wife."

"That's right," Carl said. He opened a folder and pulled out a black-and-white photograph, which he then dropped on the table. "She died in that explosion at the Kosher Deli months ago, and she was pregnant with their child. Word was put out that it was a gas explosion, but that was bullshit to keep everyone from panicking."

"Does he know the crate can't be opened?"

"Unlikely."

Will bolted out of his chair and ran for the door.

"What is it?" Carl yelled after him.

"He's going to kill them all!"

It was a gamble, a calculated risk. Will could be about to run in the front door and happen upon Said and Rollo, and then be buried by the two of them in the backyard. Instead, he found a badly beaten Rollo disassembling the explosive trigger on the crate lid while Ronald Stein stood over him, a pistol to the Russian's head. The two of them looked at Will as he walked in the door.

"Get out of here, Will," Ronald demanded the moment he saw him.

Will instinctively put his hands in the air and then lowered them.

"Ronald, you don't know the whole story; you can't do this."

"Why not? He disarms the trigger, we get the information we need, and he goes into lockup."

Will could tell by the look in Ronald's eyes that the last part was bullshit, added only for

Rollo's benefit. Ronald was going to execute him and do the same to Said.

"See that map on the wall?" Will asked, pointing to the hand-drawn map. "That's Tel Aviv, in Israel. The bomb last night was in Hamburg, and this one is here. These are all linked, different cells of the same group."

"I fucking knew it!" Rollo snapped. "I knew you were no good."

"Shut your mouth and disarm that thing!" Ronald snapped, hitting Rollo in the back of the head with the pistol. "Look, Will, I'm tired of fucking around with these assholes. This is our best option."

"I know about your wife. I know about the department."

Ronald stared at Will blankly for a moment and then steeled himself back up.

"Then you know why I can't let this pass. DFLP were the ones behind your mother's cell, and they're the ones behind this one. I just want whoever planned the bombing."

"And after you kill him? What will it bring you?"

"Nothing," Ronald answered quietly. "Which is exactly what I have now."

Looking down, Will noticed that Rollo was sweating, and realized that the Russian flawlessly disarming the security device might not be a sure thing.

"Rollo, can you really disarm that?" Will asked.

"Said put it together, but he told me how he did it." Rollo clipped a wire and then set the snips down on the floor and rested back on his knees. "Not that it matters much."

"What are you talking about?" Will asked.

The phone rang, and Rollo looked up at Will and smiled.

"Go ahead and answer it," Rollo said. "It's for you."

"Open the crate!" Ronald ordered Rollo as Will crossed the room and picked up the phone.

"Hello?"

"Hi, Will."

It was Mary Gauss on the other end.

"Mary?"

"Yes, Will, it's me. Say hello to your girlfriend."

"What?"

There was a moment of silence, and then Susanne's panicked voice came on the line.

"Will! She's crazy! She killed my father!"

"That's enough of that." Mary's voice came back on the line, calm and smooth. "By now you probably know what is in the crate."

Will looked back to see Ronald holding up two olive drab vests wired with explosives.

"You were only half right, Will, when you told me that Said told Rollo we were to be martyred. Right now Said has Maxwell's grandmother, and I have your love here. If you want her to live, you and Inspector Stein had better put your vests on."

CHAPTER 14

Ronald and Will sat silently in the backseat of Rollo's car as he drove over Portola toward Downtown. Both men wore their explosive vests beneath shirts and jackets, and no one would ever guess the danger they were in as they stood beside the two.

After they had put on the vests, Rollo instructed them to connect a plastic-coated wire across the front that armed the explosives. Presumably, if that connection broke, they would detonate. He also showed them the small handheld remote that would detonate the vests via a radio signal. The idea was that they were trading their lives for Susanne's.

"And you two thought I was the stupid one," Rollo said as he navigated the curving street. "Yet there you sit, each strapped with enough C-4 to blow up a city bus."

"Mind telling me what the point of all this is?" Ronald asked.

"I'm guessing you became a cop, Inspector Stein, because you wanted to stand up for those who could not stand up for themselves."

"No, I just like hitting people."

Rollo laughed a little.

"I doubt that. You see, Inspector, you and I are more alike than you may care to think. You stand up for those who cannot stand up for themselves, and I stand up for those who do not know enough to stand up for themselves. Each day I walk the streets of this city, surrounded by the ignorant masses, those unaware of the threat that walks amongst them."

"The Jewish threat," Will concluded.

"Not just the Jews, Will, but any parasitic race that seeks to latch itself onto another. The Jews just happen to be the most conspicuous threat." Rollo drummed his fingers on the steering wheel for a moment. "You know, Will,

I was a little hurt last night when Mary took me in the other room and told me what you two were up to. She wanted to tell me earlier but was waiting for the right time. What you two fail to understand about Mary Gauss is that she would happily put on one of those vests and do the job herself. Prison doesn't scare her, death doesn't scare her. It sounds naïve, I know, but I had hoped you and I would be friends eventually, Will."

"Is that so?" Will asked.

"Yes, it is. I've read about your grandfather and your mother and all the things they did to aid the struggle."

"Then you would also know that my grandfather killed my mother."

"I had heard that. I can't pretend to know what happened, Will, and to be honest it doesn't matter much. I judge them by their lives, not by the brief moment of their deaths."

"That's nice. What a nice world you live in, shithead." Ronald sighed.

Rollo eyed Ronald in the rearview mirror and Will could see that he was uncomfortable with Ronald's reaction. Inspector Stein was being far too nonchalant about their predicament. Originally, Randall was supposed to be the third bomber, and now he had been replaced. Will half expected Ronald to pull the connecting wire on his harness at any minute and blow them all to hell just for spite.

Will tried to think of something he could say that might sway Rollo or at least buy them some more time to come up with a plan, but it was pointless. Rollo was so far gone, so entrenched in his belief system, that there was no way to talk him out of it.

"You know I'm going to kill you... right?" Ronald said.

Rollo looked up at Ronald's reflection in the mirror. It wasn't like in the movies where the bad guy laughs and boasts about his evil plan. Rollo looked spooked, and Will couldn't blame him. Something about the way Ronald said it made the words sound like a statement of fact as opposed to a vain hope.

"I know you will try, but if I go, we will all go together."

"I wouldn't have it any other way."

"If we go through with this, how do I know you'll let Susanne go?" Will asked.

Rollo looked at him.

"She will be released, Will. You have my word. Mary wants to kill her. I know that she does, but I'll make sure she doesn't. Whatever else you may think of me, I am not a liar."

Will said nothing in response. It was pointless to debate the issue. Either way, there was nothing he could do about it.

Portola turned into Market Street, and Will realized it was the lunch hour, and people were everywhere. He had not considered that this might actually happen and that they could very possibly detonate in the middle of a crowded street, killing dozens of people.

"I'm dropping you here, Will," Rollo said, bringing the car to a stop along the side of Market Street at Golden Gate. "You're going to board the next Northbound bus and take it all the way to the terminal. Once there, you will pull your connector chord. Don't try anything stupid. I will be watching."

Rollo held up his remote detonator to demonstrate that it was not entirely necessary that Will pull the cord himself.

"I don't like busses," Ronald said in his best deadpan.

"Oh, you're not going on the bus. You're going into the Flood Building. The Anti-Defamation League has their offices on the third floor, where they print their lies and try to paint the Palestinian Freedom Fighters as murderers. You are going to go to the directory, find the office number, walk into it, and pull your cord. Remember, I can detonate you any time I choose. If it's any comfort, you'll be killing fewer people if you do what I tell you than if I were to just do it right here and now."

"What's the office number?" Ronald asked.

"Just go to the third floor. You'll see it."

"Wait a minute," Ronald said with the beginnings of a smirk. "You don't know their office number?" Rollo scowled at him. "You didn't plan this very well, did you?"

"Fuck you; how's that for a plan?" Rollo snapped. "Get out of the car and start walking."

"I just think it's funny that you don't know the office number, that's all. No hard feelings."

Ronald looked to Will.

"Do you want some gum?" he asked.

"What?" Will replied, finding it hard to believe Ronald was offering him gum.

"Here, take it," he said, handing Will three foil wrapped sticks of gum. "For fresh breath."

"Are you insane?"

Ronald pressed them into Will's palm and opened his door.

"Save them for later," he said and pointed at the vest.

With that, Ronald shut the door and walked briskly down Market Street as if he didn't have a care in the world.

"You too, get going." Rollo said. "Enjoy your gum."

Opening his door, Will Hessler stepped out and walked a dozen feet to the bus stop. It felt as if everyone was watching him, as if they knew what was about to happen.

Standing at the bus stop, Will's mind was running a hundred miles an hour. Absurdly enough, he was trying to figure out what the third target would be so that he would know where Maxwell was going. If he somehow managed to keep himself from exploding on a bus full of people, he would then try to stop Maxwell.

It came to him in a flash. The Israeli Embassy on Montgomery Street. Will saw a payphone on the sidewalk and considered trying to use it when he saw the arriving bus roll to a stop. Across the street he could see Rollo staring at him from the car.

The doors opened and Will followed the line of people up the steps and onto the bus, dropping his fare as he went. He unbuttoned the shirt he was wearing over the vest and looked at the thing. Small packs of explosives were secured in the ammo pouch pockets, and wires were sewn into the lining, running from the explosives to the detonator. A small antenna sprouted from the detonator to receive the signal. When he was much younger a friend had tried to get him interested in radios, and Will now wished he had pursued the hobby so he would at least have an idea of what he was dealing with. Surveying the vest, he unconsciously removed one of the sticks of gum Ronald had given him, unwrapped it and chewed it. He crumpled the wrapper in his hand and looked at it.

Will flashed back to Ronald pointing at him in the car. He had not yet fully buttoned up his shirt. Ronald was pointing at the antennae.

The wrapper. Foil. Foil blocks radio signals. It couldn't be that simple.

Will unwrapped the other two sticks of gum and began chewing them. The gum was the sealant to hold the foil in place. He chewed furiously to ensure the gum was completely malleable before removing it from his mouth. He then carefully molded the gum around the small antenna, covering not only the wire, but the base and a good portion of the top of the detonator. Next the foil was applied, also covering the antenna.

There was no time to think about whether or not this was actually going to work. Reaching up, Will yanked on the wire to stop the bus. They were still a block from the next stop, precious minutes he didn't have.

"Stop the bus!" Will shouted. The bus driver looked up into his rearview mirror but did not stop. Will shouted again, "Stop this bus!"

Still nothing. Grabbing two of the rest supports, Will leaned back and drove a foot through the window.

"Hey!" The bus driver yelled and hit the brakes so hard Will was knocked off of his feet

330 / JORDAN VEZINA

and to the floor. He rebounded quickly and shoved his way out the rear doors and onto Market Street.

There wasn't much point in trying to get to Ronald, as he must have already known what it had taken Will some time to figure out, so he decided to hang everything on his best guess as to where they would send Maxwell with the third vest and sprinted toward Montgomery Street.

After he hit the switch on his detonator, Rollo stood outside of the Flood Building for a few minutes before finally venturing inside. Initially, he had given Ronald five minutes after the inspector entered to detonate himself. Then Rollo was unpleasantly surprised by the failure of his 'failsafe' device. Matters worsened when people began exiting the building in an orderly fashion, in the way that people are instructed to in an emergency.

Roland Federov felt a shot of cold fear down his spine that he had not experienced in quite some time. He was not afraid of Ronald or even of what Said Al Assan would do to him if this plan failed. He was afraid that all of his work to reach this point was about to go up in smoke, and not in the way he had intended.

Rollo moved through the lobby quickly but carefully, watching for anyone hiding around a corner. Stupidly, he had left his pistol in the car, not expecting to need it, as anyone he considered a possible threat was strapped with explosives. He had also become so used to physically intimidating everyone that he rarely felt the need for any weapon but his fists. As he bounded up the stairs, he remembered the look in Inspector Stein's eyes, the total lack of fear, and the promise he had made.

In the upstairs hallway, Rollo saw the door to the offices of the ADL half open.

"Are you in there, Inspector?"

"Stop being a pussy Rollo and get in here."

Rollo bristled at that and instinctively shoved the door open and walked in. What he found was the former Inspector Stein sitting on a desk smoking a cigarette. Ronald was trying to appear calm and casual, but there was no mistaking the rage in his eyes. Beside Ronald on the desk sat the suicide bomber vest, folded neatly.

"Impressive," Rollo said.

"Not really." Ronald answered as if speaking to an ignorant child. "If any of you dumbasses had taken five minutes to check up on me, you would have known I did four years in the Marine Corps in Explosive Ordinance Disposal and then another five on SFPD bomb squad."

Rollo's face was emotionless.

"Right about now you're wondering what's going to happen next?" Ronald asked.

"We are men of action, Inspector. We do not waste our time talking."

Reaching down, Ronald put out his cigarette and stood up.

"Then let's get on with it."

Will was nearly to Montgomery Street when he noticed something he had not been expecting. Rollo's car was parked next to the curb. Will stopped suddenly, half expecting to see the Russian jump out of it, but quickly realized that for some reason it had been abandoned.

Pulling open the passenger side door, Will

reached into the glove box to find exactly what he had been expecting. Rollo's pistol fell into his hand, and he shoved it as far as it would go into his pocket. He searched further through the car, hoping to find the keys, but to no avail. Instead he found the hand-drawn map that had been on the wall in Rollo's house, now wrapped in a clear plastic bag. Will stuck it in his other pocket and bolted from the car, running for all he was worth up Market and onto Montgomery.

Will Hessler had never been an athlete, but he ran as hard as he could toward the Israeli Embassy. He was sweating like a pig, and felt as if his lungs were full of acid when he finally came to a stop.

Maxwell was already there, standing at the gate.

"Stop!" Will shouted.

Maxwell turned, and Will saw the raw fear in his eyes.

"Will? What are you doing here?"

"They tried to do the same thing to me. They have Susanne!"

"Will, get out of here! I have to do this." Maxwell was resigned to his fate, still frightened by what he was about to do, but accepting that there was no alternative.

"She'll know, Maxwell!"

"What?"

"Your grandmother. She'll know what you did! Do you want her to know all of these people had to die so that she could live?"

Maxwell turned away from the gate and looked at Will.

"You don't understand, Will. She raised me. She did everything she could for me. I can't let that animal kill her."

"Maxwell, I'm sure Ronald is on his way there right now; you just have to give us time!"

Behind Maxwell, the Israeli security guards at the gate were shouting into their radios with their weapons at the ready. They knew something was about to happen.

As if in slow motion, Maxwell removed his jacket to reveal his bomb vest and turned toward the embassy gate. He may not have meant it to be a threat, but the guards took it as such, and they lunged forward with their weapons sighted on him.

The sub-machine gun rounds stitched Maxwell's body, several entering his head until it came apart. One nicked the side of Will's head, and another passed cleanly through the right side of his torso, just a half inch in. At the time he didn't even realize it.

"No! Goddammit!" Will screamed at the guards, but they held fast without emotion, now with their weapons trained on him. For a moment Will wondered why they weren't coming after him, but then realized they could not leave the Consulate grounds, and he was not clearly armed, as Maxwell had been. Will reached into his pocket (lucky not to have been shot doing it), removed the map, and threw it over the fence.

"There are more bombs in Tel Aviv!" he shouted at them angrily.

There was no time. To his right he saw a man in a business suit unlocking his car, and it was as if Will Hessler's body was moving independent of his mind as he pulled out the pistol and put it to the man's head.

"I'm sorry, I'm so sorry, but I need your car!"

Will felt horrible about taking that man's car,

but either way he was now speeding down Broadway, running red lights and quickly losing track of how many times he was nearly hit by other drivers. For the first time in his life, there wasn't a cop in sight, and all he wanted was to see those flashing lights behind him.

Will was never one of those people who knew every twist and turn of San Francisco, and was doing a lot of guesswork as he made his way toward the Presidio. Moreover, he really hoped he was right about Ronald disabling the device. Will's actions at the embassy had most likely handed Maxwell's grandmother a death sentence, but there had been no other move to make.

The Bonafide house was right outside of the Presidio on North Point Street, blocks away from any armed sentry that might have offered help. It would only be an extra five minutes to find one, but it was very possible that those would be five minutes Will could not spare, and Susanne did not have.

Will stopped a block away from the house and cut the engine. He sat for a moment and recognized how dead quiet the neighborhood was. Will didn't know much about guns, but he knew enough to pop out the wheel of the pistol and check for rounds. Reaching down to the floor, he picked up a discarded paper bag and stuffed the gun inside of it. He looked down at himself and became aware again that he was wearing a bomb.

The air was cool on his face and sweat soaked body as it blew into the gaps between the clothes and the vest. No one gave him a second look as he walked briskly down North Point wearing a suicide bomber vest and holding a gun inside of a paper bag. Susanne's house was getting closer by the minute and he had no idea what he was going to do.

"Get up, we're going."

Looking up at Ronald, Rollo spit some blood and teeth onto the floor and grimaced. He looked down at the suicide bomber vest Ronald had secured to him after he felt the man had taken enough of a beating.

"Fuck you," Rollo responded.

"I'm not playing with you."

Reaching down, Ronald took one of Rollo's hands and broke his ring finger with a sick snapping sound. Rollo cried out and leapt to his feet, some broken thing in his right knee grinding as he moved. Ronald was barely keeping his anger in check, and shoving Rollo into the wall, punched the man in the back of the head several times before grabbing him and throwing him into the hallway. Rollo hit the wall and fell to the floor, obviously disoriented.

"Get up!" Ronald shouted, but Rollo just lay there, obviously having a hard time focusing on anything.

Raising his leg, Ronald began stomping on Rollo's head and neck until the Russian got the message and struggled to his feet amid the flurry of blows.

"Where's your car, shithead?"

As quietly as he could, Will slipped over the fence and around the side of the Bonafide house into the backyard. He knew Carl kept a key beneath the mat on the back porch, and hopefully he could get into the house without Mary hearing.

Will froze. He felt himself starting to shake as he saw the body lying in the grass and he had to make a supreme effort to get himself under control. A blanket had been thrown over the body, but Carl Bonafide's hand was hanging out from underneath it, leaving little mystery as to who it was.

Will removed a key from beneath the mat. Every sound was amplified a hundred times, and the noise of the tumblers clicking inside the lock mechanism seemed to him as if they could be heard from across the street. Once the door had unlatched; Will crouched down, and let the paper bag covering the gun fall to the ground as walked into the laundry room.

He could partially see into the kitchen, and there was Susanne sitting on a chair. Will couldn't see where Mary Gauss was. He developed a hasty plan in his mind to run into the kitchen and put himself between Susanne and where he imagined Mary to be.

Will crept down the short hallway from the laundry room. He heard the picture frame hit the floor before realizing that his shoulder had knocked it off of the shelf.

Ronald walked Rollo out of the Flood Building

to where the car was parked, and gestured for him to get in the driver side seat. Rollo complied, and Ronald slid into the back.

Rollo hesitated for a moment, and then moved quickly, opening the glove box and reaching inside for the gun that wasn't there, the pistol that Will Hessler had taken. Ronald replied to this action by punching Rollo again in the back of the head, then reaching forward Ronald put him in a chokehold.

"Maxwell's mother, is she alive?"

"Dead," Rollo managed to grunt.

"Any other guns in the car?"

Rollo hesitated, and Ronald applied more pressure to his windpipe.

"A shotgun, in the trunk."

"Good. We're going for a little drive. It's time to pay that friend of yours a visit."

"You're going to kill me, aren't you?" Rollo asked as he started the car.

"If you're lucky."

"I refuse to die by the hand of a Jew."

Reaching down, Rollo grabbed the dead man's cord connecting the two sides of the bomb vest he was wearing and broke it.

· · ·

Will lunged into the kitchen in time to see Mary grab Susanne and put the gun to her head.

"Don't move, you fucking bitch!" Mary shouted in Susanne's ear.

"Let her go!"

"Where's Rollo?" Mary snapped.

"Dead." Will tried to steady his pistol hand.

"I doubt it. Look at you, Will, you're trembling. You're not going to be the hero today," Mary said mockingly.

"This is over with, Mary! I stopped Maxwell at the consulate and gave them the Tel Aviv map. The police will be here soon."

Mary studied him for a moment and then smiled.

"No, they won't. No one knows you're here, do they, Will? You're all alone."

Will said nothing, only kept his gun on her.

"Can you even shoot that straight, Will? I can shoot mine, but I don't think you can. I think you're more likely to hit her," Mary said, pulling back the hammer on her Beretta pistol.

"Fine," Will said, and grabbed the dead man's cord to the vest in his left hand. "But if she dies, it's going to be by my hand, not yours!"

. . .

"I disabled it," Ronald said. "You think I didn't figure you'd try something like that? You're not getting off that easy. The only way that thing's going off is if I trigger it."

Any sense of hope Rollo had was gone as he pulled into the driveway of the house on Parker Street that Said had rented.

Ronald stood directly behind Rollo with the shotgun pointed at the door as Federov rang the bell. After a moment the door opened a few inches and a face could be seen peering out.

"Try to run and I will shoot you down," Ronald said conversationally.

For a moment it seemed as if Said might try to run, but he thought better of it, and opened the door the rest of the way. Said looked Rollo over, seemingly in disbelief at the man's condition. Rollo shuffled in the door completely broken, with Ronald behind him. Ronald closed the door and stood a few feet away from the two men.

"What is this about officer?" Said asked innocently. "What has happened to this man?"

"Knock it off!" Ronald snapped. "Is the grandmother really dead?"

"What are you talking about?" Said asked, looking concerned.

Ronald covered the few feet between them in a split second and slammed the butt of the shotgun square into Said's head. The man crashed to the floor holding his face, blood dripping between his fingers.

"What are you doing?" Said shouted.

"Kneel!" Ronald yelled back, putting the shotgun to Said's head.

"I am but a simple Lebanese business man! Why are you doing this to me? You are a police officer!"

"Not anymore," Ronald hissed.

"Please, I do not understand. I did nothing wrong!"

"Neither did my sister... or my wife and child, you son of a bitch."

Rollo jumped back as the sound of thunder filled the room and a headless Said fell to the floor.

Ronald racked another round into the chamber and trained the shotgun on Rollo.

"Get on your knees."

Rollo stared defiantly at Ronald. "You will have to shoot me standing, like a man."

Anther shotgun blast sent Rollo into the wall and then to the floor. Ronald walked to the body and emptied his remaining six rounds into it. He dropped the shotgun and looked at his hands. They were shaking.

The room was silent again. The two bodies lay on the floor, Said headless and most of Rollo's torso destroyed.

"It's over," Ronald whispered to himself, if for no other reason than to break the silence.

Walking down the hallway, Ronald located the phone and put in a call to the SFPD, apprising them of his and William Hessler's situation. Already he heard sirens in the distance, most likely responding to the gunshots.

A chair in the living room seemed like it would be particularly comfortable, and so Ronald sat down in it. Looking down the hall-way, he could see Rollo and Said's bodies in the entryway. There was a sense of finality to the whole thing that he found disturbing. Reaching into his coat pocket, Ronald removed the remote detonator and slowly pulled out the short antenna. This had been the plan. Do the job, eliminate the threats, and then leave this world. Ronald's thumb hovered over the trigger, then his hand began to shake again, and the detonator fell to the floor. For the first time since their deaths, Ronald cried in the darkness over the loss of his wife and unborn child.

"You don't have the balls to do it, Will," Mary said. "You don't have what it takes to kill someone."

"You can walk away, Mary. You can walk out of this house and go to Mexico or wherever you want and no one will ever find you."

They circled the room like some macabre dance, Mary dragging Susanne with her.

"What good does that do me, Will? Getting away isn't what I wanted. You and your Jew cop took away the only thing I wanted. So maybe now I should take away the only thing you want?"

Mary looked Susanne over. Susanne's eyes were fixed on Will. She seemed to be waiting for him to do something.

"Will... what is it about her that you love? What is it she has that I don't?"

"A soul."

"You always did have a clever comeback. So, I can just walk away?"

"Yes."

"Even though I bashed her Daddy's head in with a baseball bat? You're just going to let me walk out of here?"

Will's eyes went to Susanne's, but he could not decode what she was thinking.

"You can walk away," he said slowly.

"I would need a distraction." Mary walked behind Susanne and stepped away from her, still holding the gun to her head. "This is what happens when you play games with a woman's emotions, Will."

"No!"

Mary fired three quick shots, and the bullets ripped through Susanne as the girl stumbled forward. Will caught her and became aware of the warmth of her blood on his face. By the time he looked up, Mary was gone. Will understood why Mary had not tried to shoot him. She wanted Susanne to die and for him to have to live with it.

Sitting on the floor, Will held Susanne in his arms as she bled and trembled.

"I'm dying," she whispered.

"No, you're not."

Will flashed back to Isabelle dying in his arms. It was happening again.

"I am, Will." Her breathing was becoming labored. "I love you. More than anyone ever has or ever will."

"You're not dying. I love you."

Reaching up with a shaking hand, she touched the side of his face.

"There was nothing you could have done," Susanne whispered.

There was a crash at the front door and Will looked up to see paramedics running down the hallway. One pulled him away as the other started working on Susanne. Will wanted to stay with her, but Ronald Stein grabbed him by the arm and walked him out the front door.

"We have to give them room to work," Ronald said. "Look at me, Will!"

Will managed to focus and looked at Ronald.

"I need you to be calm, do you understand?"

Will realized that he was crying and shaking and worked hard to calm himself down. Looking to his right, he saw Mary Gauss sitting on the lawn, hands cuffed behind her back and her face covered in blood. Will lunged at her with a guttural sound like an animal and was yanked off of his feet and pinned to the side of the house by Ronald.

"Calm down, Will! This won't do any good!"

He struggled for a moment and finally relented.

"Will, you've been shot. You need medical attention."

At that point, from a combination of blood loss, stress, and exhaustion, Will passed out.

"Where the fuck are you going?"

Ronald Stein had been unable to resist punching Mary Gauss in the face when he saw her come running around the corner of the house and nearly into him. It was not a soft punch either, pulled in consideration of the fact that she was a woman. It had been a hard, angry punch, hitting her the way he would hit a man he hated, a man he wanted to kill.

That single punch became a turning point for Ronald to begin his healing and rebuilding process. It had been the culmination of his building rage, but in the immediate aftermath, he realized it was not the right thing to do. Indeed, Mary Gauss deserved it, but Ronald felt dirty and like less of a man because of it.

As Ronald pulled up with the police and EMS units, he heard the shots in the house and was afraid he was too late. In some ways he had been.

Maxwell and his grandmother were both dead. Carl Bonafide was also dead of blunt trauma to his skull, courtesy of Mary Gauss. After extensive interrogation, Mary explained why she had not just shot Susanne Bonafide and left.

"I wanted to know what she had that I didn't. I wanted to know why Will loved her and not me."

Susanne took four rounds point blank, collapsing one of her lungs, rupturing her appendix, shattering her left hipbone, and one lodging in her leg. It would take several surgeries to put her back together, complete with an artificial hip that allowed her to regain near full mobility, but she would have to walk with a cane for the rest of her life due to nerve damage. The round that had entered her right leg was left inside, as the risk of trying to remove it outweighed any benefits.

Susanne never felt sorry for herself or became angry over the situation. Susanne Bonafide was just thankful that she and Will were both alive and still together.

She would even joke about it, "Look on the bright side, I have more time in surgery now than any other med student."

Will was always concerned that she did not grieve her father more publicly, but accepted that Susanne regarded that as a private thing, not for the eyes of others. He knew that in the past he had dealt with loss in the same way and was often assailed by others as bottling up his emotions and not dealing with them.

Two months passed as the summer wound to a close. Ronald was re-instated in the San Francisco Police Department, his actions over the past year quietly swept under the rug. He was given no awards but also no reprimands.

Will Hessler was debriefed extensively by a CIA agent who had apparently been a friend of Carl Bonafide's. This man seemed to know absolutely nothing about what had happened, and Will was curious as to how much Carl had told the agency about him, but couldn't seem to get an answer. Will suspected that this was because Carl had been true to his word and kept him off of the radar as much as possible. Will was in the office with the agent for days, arriving at eight in the morning and sometimes not leaving until midnight. He sat and stared at photos of known DFLP members and technical specs on different suicide bomber vests so they could try to track who had made them. He read the rap sheets on every Russian Mafia member in San Francisco and every Nazi war criminal still walking the earth. There was actually a point where he became concerned he was going to be conscripted.

Perhaps it was ego, but Will was a little disappointed that they finally did send him on his way and made no effort to recruit him. He had no desire to work for the CIA, but it would have been a thoughtful gesture.

Will half-expected Saul Greenbaum to appear at the foot of his bed in the middle of the night, but he never did. As time went on, Will accepted that Saul's use for him had ended and that was all there was to it.

Ronald and Will attended Rollo's burial. Neither of them were quite sure why they did this. Despite everything the Russian had done, Will viewed Rollo as being sort of a tragic character, jumping from the orphanage to the prison system, always living a life of violence and then indoctrinated into a belief system of monster logic from which he would never break free. Will did not labor under the delusion that deep down Rollo was a good person, but in some ways he saw a lot of his mother in him. If she had not grown up the way she had, perhaps things could have been different.

Or maybe he was just an evil son of a bitch.

"I'm sorry I used you, Will."

Will and Ronald sat in a pub on Stanyan Street the night of Rollo's burial, drinking and talking about what had transpired over the past several months.

"I won't pretend it doesn't bother me."

Ronald nodded.

"I was blinded by my rage, by my desire for revenge," Ronald said. "It started after my wife died in the deli bombing. I was with her in the hospital. There wasn't any doubt that she would die, but it didn't happen right away. I had to wait a few days. They tried to save the baby... they thought they could save him, but they couldn't."

"We don't have to talk about this, Ronald."

"No, I do." It was obvious by his expression that the explanation was as much for him as it was for Will. "I should have watched out for you more, kept you out of it."

"Ronald, if I hadn't gotten mixed up in this, a lot more people would have died. Whether or not you did it for the right reasons, in the end it was the right thing."

Ronald looked away and took a drink of his beer.

"I used to put a gun to my head every night. I would sit down at my kitchen table, open a bottle of bourbon, and just put my gun to my head over and over. I don't know why, I just did. Ever since I killed Said and Rollo I haven't done that. I can sleep now. For what that's worth."

Will didn't know what to say. He knew how he felt having lost someone he loved, but it's different for everyone. The subtleties of love and loss are the hobgoblins of human emotion.

It was a cool fall evening on the wharf as Will stood outside the gallery smoking a cigarette, one of the hundreds that he would routinely declare was his last. For whatever reason, over the past few weeks he had begun having nightmares, haunted by images of his loved ones dying violently. He was also missing Isabelle. Caught up in those dreams, he was with her again and everything else was gone. Then he would awaken beside Susanne and have a flash of horrible sadness, first at realizing it was a dream and Isabelle was gone, directly followed by guilt over missing her. It made him question his fidelity to Susanne, but over time he realized that dreams do not define who we are and that mourning and loss are two beasts that require time to satiate their hunger.

As per the usual, the wharf was crowded by tourists. Will watched them milling about, smiling, laughing, and walking with family and friends.

"They sleep the sleep of the innocent," a rough voice said from beside him. Will turned to see Saul Greenbaum standing a few feet from him on the street.

"That's how it should be," Will replied.

Saul nodded.

"It is true. Often, we become so caught up in our business that we forget we do it so that they don't have to. The few must sacrifice so that the many may live in peace."

"I can only assume you're not speaking in the abstract."

"We Jews cannot afford such luxuries, Will, so no I am not."

"I have to admit I was wondering what happened to you."

"I was caught up in business, Will. It was nothing personal. I wanted very much to speak with you before now and to thank you." Reaching out, Saul shook Will's hand. "The nation of Israel owes you a debt that we can never repay."

"No payment necessary, Saul. It was the right thing to do."

Saul stared at Will hard for a moment as if trying to assess something.

"Yet still, that does not mean we are hesitant to continue running a tab."

"How so?" Will asked, regarding him coolly.

"Without having had any training, you are already one of the most effective operatives I have ever met, and you are not yet old enough to drink. Your services would be highly valued by my agency."

"That's not my life, Saul."

"But it is who you are."

"What do you know about me, Saul Greenbaum? Really? I'm an artist, not some secret agent. I was pulled into this business against my will. I want to live a normal life."

"You can have a normal life."

"Not like this I can't! Because of this— because of your war—my girlfriend has a hip replacement and walks with a cane. She cries herself to sleep most nights because of the pain from the bullet still in her leg!"

"My family..." Saul's voice trailed off. He looked at the ground for a moment and then back to Will. His eyes were wet. "They were taken from me during the war. I escaped and fought with the resistance in the Rudninkai Forest and elsewhere, with Abba Kovner. My family was confined to Kaunas, where they died, all but one. When I returned, I found my brother still alive, but I heard the stories about him, that he had served the Nazis, that he had been complicit. He confessed all of this to me, begged for forgiveness, begged for mercy. I did show him mercy, by shooting him in the street. Having to live with himself would have been a much crueler fate."

Saul stuffed his hands in his pockets and looked around at the people passing him by on the street. From his pocket he produced one of his cards and pressed it into Will's palm.

"The world is a horrible place, Will Hessler, and men are the machines that may give that horror pause. It is up to you, and you alone, to decide if you are such a man"

· · ·

"You've been quiet."

Susanne's words broke Will out of his thoughts, and he saw her staring at him from the other side of the dinner table. Her father's house was eerily quiet, only the sounds of forks and knives on plates, and thoughtful breathing.

"Yes. Saul Greenbaum came to see me the other night at the gallery."

There was a shot of fear in her eyes.

"What did he want?"

"You know what he wanted, Susanne."

"What did you say?"

Will realized that he did not know what his answer was.

"I told him no. I told him it wasn't my life."

Susanne nodded.

"Do you think that's true?" she asked.

Will was taken aback by the question and by the way that she wasn't staring at him but into him.

"What do you mean?"

"Sometimes, Will, who we are is not necessarily who we would have chosen to be. On occasion, circumstance dictates who we become. I feel like... maybe no one has told you that you're a hero."

"Susanne, it's not that simple."

"Let me finish. It's not because you're a perfect person, or because you're better than anyone else. It's because you put others before yourself. It's because you stood to gain nothing from your actions; you didn't have to do the things you did. Have you thought about what you did at the Israeli Embassy? You could have just come straight here for me, but you went out of your way and put both of us at risk to help save the lives of complete strangers. That's not something you can just turn off."

Will was embarrassed to hear those things. He knew they were true, but at the same time they made him feel strange.

"I'm not trying to tell you which way to go, Will. The idea of you doing this full-time scares the hell out of me, but I have to acknowledge that you're one of the few men who can do it."

"I know."

"Whatever you decide, Will, I'll support you." Susanne stood up, took her cane, and smiled. "And I'm getting more wine."

Susanne stopped beside him, and her hand gripped the cane until her knuckles turned white. Will looked up, and she was gritting her teeth, a tear rolling down her cheek.

"What's wrong?" Will asked, standing up and holding her.

"My leg. I'm sorry, Will, I can feel the bullet."

"Don't be sorry; it's not your fault."

Will Hessler held her close to him as she cried, and in that moment he knew the answer to Saul's question.

One Year Later

The Top Hat Bar
Los Angeles, California
October 19, 1977

J urgen Steiner sat in a darkened corner of the run down L.A. bar, keeping to himself while at the same time staying acutely aware of who was coming and going from the establishment. This was important for two reasons.

The first, was that Jurgen was (through a shell corporation) the owner of the Top Hat. He had found this to be advantageous in terms of laundering the not insignificant amount of Nazi gold he still held in several numbered Swiss bank accounts.

The second reason was that he was a machine which could not rest. He could not and would not. He had seen the importance of this mindset himself on the Eastern Front, during his short time commanding German soldiers in battle before being tapped for counter-intelligence work.

In war a man could not let up, not for even a single moment. Those who did would find themselves being counseled by their maker, and far sooner than they might like. He had seen many men die because of a momentary lapse in vigilance.

This was why he always held court at this same corner table, facing every entrance.

Through one of these entrances he saw a man walk into the bar. He was big, probably one of the biggest men Jurgen had ever seen.

He easily stood six foot six and was at least three hundred pounds. While he had some extra weight around the midsection, he was not fat. This was a man who was used to getting what he wanted and forcing other men to submit to his will.

This man walked through the dimly lit bar, scanning the patrons, and finally his eyes fell upon Jurgen Steiner. He smiled nervously and continued to walk forward. Another man stepped from the shadows and held up a hand.

"You are?" Heinrich Weber asked.

"Michael Reiner," the big man answered. He was taken aback for a moment by this man's prosthetic nose. He looked to be about the same age as Jurgen, and Michael wondered if this man was also a former member of the Third Reich. "I have a meeting with Mister Cavalogne."

This was the pseudonym that Jurgen had adopted during his time in Los Angeles, Rico Cavalogne. While it was unlikely there were Israeli intelligence agents hiding around every corner who would recognize the name "Jurgen Steiner" it would be foolish to be brazenly open about his identity. That fool Franklin Hessler had made this mistake, and it had led him to ruin. True, no one had 'outed' him, but it had been a symptom of his arrogance.

"Do you now?" Weber asked with a sick smile. "Tell me then, Mister Reiner. Where does the power lie?"

Michael remembered the challenge question from his written correspondence with this Rico Cavalogne. The ad in the Portland Tribune classifieds had caught the attention of one of his lieutenants in The Rising Storm. They had then discovered that the advertisement had also circulated through a dozen other newspapers in the Pacific Northwest.

It was in a code, but it was a code that any white supremacist would understand. Not only was it a code, it was a call to actions.

Numerology club now recruiting for future plans. Fans of the numbers 318 and 88 encouraged to apply.

Three-eighteen stood for the Third Reich and Eighty-Eight (H being the eighth letter in the alphabet) referred to the Nazi greeting of "Heil Hitler". When this was brought to his attention, Michael Reiner knew what it meant. He understood the call to action.

It had only taken a handful of letters with this Rico Cavalogne to convince Michael that he was the real deal. This man was a hardcore former SS commander who going to make a play, something big and he needed an Army to do it.

Michael Reiner had an army. Yes, the membership of The Rising Storm wasn't what is used to be, but it was still quite healthy. Healthy enough that he would be a useful addition to the plans of a man like Rico Cavalogne.

"Where does the power lie?" Michael repeated the question. "In the sons of the Motherland."

Heinrich nodded his approval of this answer and motioned to where Jurgen Steiner sat.

Michael Reiner walked the remaining dozen steps to the large table and stopped. He wasn't sure how he should address this man. It was a new experience for the giant, as he was used to being the king holding court, not approaching one.

"Mister Cavalogne," Reiner said. "My name is Michael Reiner."

"Please, Mister Reiner. Have a seat," Jurgen said with a broad smile, gesturing to the chair across from him. "And please, call me Jurgen Steiner. I believe we are at a point where we can dispense with this 'Rico Cavalogne' business."

Michael returned the smile as best he could, as smiling had never felt natural to him. Much like laughing at jokes or feeling empathy. He understood what these emotions and facial cues meant, but they had always felt strange, like wearing a coat that does not quite fit.

Jurgen Steiner was in his early fifties, but quite fit and with a certain sense of what could only be described as "friendly menace" about him. To the untrained eye he had a ready smile and laugh lines that implied a life full of joy. To the eye that knew better, these attributes were a mask. A mask to hide the face of a beast that was quite sensitized to the sensation of bones breaking between its teeth.

Jurgen studied Michael Reiner for a

moment from behold cold, light blue eyes, and then smoothed his grey/white hair back with one hand before allowing his posture to relax. Michael knew that this man had been ready to take his life, had things not gone as expected.

"Thank you for agreeing to see me," Michael said.

"Of course," Jurgen replied as he waved to the bartender and held up two fingers. "I assume that you are a whisky man?"

Michael smiled.

"I'm a proud white man. Could I be anything else?"

Jurgen laughed out loud at this.

The bartender approached the table with two glasses and a bottle of Black Forest-Rothaus Whisky.

"Do you know this brand?" Jurgen asked as the bartender poured three fingers into each glass.

"I don't believe I do," Michael replied.

"It's a German whisky. Depending on who you ask, 'whisky' is spelled with or without an 'e', but in Germany, we say it differently. It's 'whesskey'. Because it is produced in the state of Hesse. Though this one was produced in

Baden. It is one of the oldest distilleries, originally for Schnapps, but it has been repurposed."

Jurgen lifted his glass and gestured for Michael to do the same.

Both men took a drink. Michael smiled.

"It's good," Michael said.

"That's power you're tasting," Jurgen said as he set his glass down. "That's history. Reiner is a German name, correct?"

"Yes, it is. My mother and father were both from Germany."

"Did they serve?"

Michael's face changed.

"No, they did not."

"Why?" Jurgen asked, his curiosity piqued.

"My father believed that serving the Motherland would mean certain death. He was a coward."

"Do not be so hard on him," Jurgen chastised the man. "No one can know what lurks within the hearts of men. I have a granddaughter who sought to chase the Fuhrer's dream. I would have moved mountains to turn her away from it."

"Why?" Michael asked. "If you don't mind me asking."

"Mister Reiner, we do the things we do so that our children will not have to. We fight this battle today, in the shadows, using anonymous ads and guerrilla tactics, so that our grandchildren will not be fighting the same battle. For if they do, it will be like Berlin in nineteen forty-five all over again. Fighting the unclean in the streets with sticks and bricks."

"I understand."

"Good." Jurgen paused for a moment. "I assume by your presence here that you are prepared to commit yourself to the cause?"

"I am."

"My cause?" Jurgen pushed.

"I am."

"What do you bring to the table?"

"We're sixty strong, with forty fighters."

Jurgen smiled at this.

"Forty fighters?"

"Yes," Michael said.

"What of the other twenty?"

Michael seemed uncomfortable.

"Women and children. Camp followers."

"In Berlin, do you know what percentage of the citizenry were figures?" Jurgen asked.

"No, sir."

"One hundred percent," Jurgen said. "So I ask again, how many fighters do you have?"

"Sixty."

"Excellent."

Michael Reiner met Heinrich Weber by the door.

"He's the real deal," Michael said.

"Indeed," Heinrich said. "You won't see me again. I am only here for a short time to help my old friend with this project. He will meet you again in San Francisco at this address on the date and time written."

Heinrich handed Michael a slip of paper, which Michael pocketed.

"What do I do until then?"

Heinrich handed Michael a large envelope. There was something heavy inside of it.

"I need you to put this in a bathroom north of San Francisco."

Kezar's Pub
San Francisco, California
October 19, 1977

Jacob Mitzak sat across from Jane Sutcliffe at the small table in Kezar's pub, neither one saying a word. Jane occasionally glared at Jacob, and he in return pretended that she was not there. This made the most illogical sense, as they were not on speaking terms at that moment.

The two had been in an on again/ off again relationship for the previous twenty years, the intensity of which had been sufficient at one point to bear them a daughter. That intensity however (like any explosion) eventually waned.

Saul Greenbaum returned from the bar with three glasses of whisky and set one in front of Jacob, the other in front of Jane and reserved one for himself as he took his seat.

"Are we still not on speaking terms?" Saul asked.

Jacob looked at Saul coldly.

"I'll take that as a 'yes'," Saul said.

"Perhaps if one of us could get his arrested development under control," Jane said sharply. "We wouldn't keep having these problems."

"Saul," Jacob said. "Tell Miss Sutcliffe that—"

"No," Saul interrupted him. "I'm not doing this again. You are two of the top intelligence operatives Mossad has in its arsenal, yet you insist on behaving like children when you're together. Either that or disappearing into a broom closet together. Are you unable to work together? If so, tell me now."

"He—" Jane started, but Saul held up a hand to silence her.

"I do not want to hear it," Saul insisted. "Yes or no. Can you work together?"

Jane turned to Jacob and then back to Saul.

"No," she said pointedly.

What in the hell did he do this time? Saul wondered to himself.

"Fine. I need him here, you know that," Saul said. "So I want you to stand by in Vancouver for the inevitable extraction."

Jane wanted to argue, to insist that she should be the one to stay, but she grudgingly had to admit that Jacob "The Hammer of

Israel" Mitzak was the better operative for this particular job.

"I understand," Jane said. "I'll be on a plane tonight and have everything in place."

"Good," Saul said and turned to Jacob. "And you. You understand what you need to do?"

"I still think there must be someone better suited for this. I thought Commander Fine was supposed to handle his training?"

"Once we're back in Israel, yes, but we need to screen him first. If he cannot stand up to your... methods, it would be a waste of time to bring him all the way back to Haifa."

"I've never trained anyone before."

"And you never will if you don't get this first one under your belt."

"What about the warrants?" Jacob asked. "Interpol is still looking for me."

"But not the San Francisco Police Department. Even if you somehow managed to get yourself detained, it is unlikely that they would think to run you through Interpol."

"Unlikely but not impossible," Jacob corrected him.

"Agreed," Saul acquiesced. "But you didn't

get into this business because you crave a safe life."

"Like I had a choice."

"Like you'd have it any other way," Saul said with a smile.

"Do I have execute authority?" Jane asked.

"Why do you need execute authority?" Saul asked.

"Because I want it. I don't want to be left dangling out in the wind waiting for approval from you to take action."

Saul thought about this. Lately, Jane had begun taking her call sign "Avenger 3/1" a little too literally. He suspected her of executing several assets that she felt were not contrite enough about their past actions for her tastes. This included the woman in Argentina who had "escaped" Jane's custody.

The problem was that he could not actually prove anything, he only had suspicions. Even if he did have concrete proof, would he do anything with it? Jane, like Jacob was an indispensable operative in Saul's black operations arm of the Mossad known only as The Box. Finding agents who would not only be willing to do the work he asked, but would excel at it was no easy task. This kind of work frayed the edges of one's soul, and it never took long for an agent to start coming apart at the seams.

Perhaps that was what was happening to Jane. She was coming apart at the seams. The scarcity of agents like her, however, meant that Saul would need to see her unravel quite a bit more before he pulled her from the field.

"You can have it once you touch down in the desert, but not in Canada and not here."

Jane glared at Saul for a moment and then relented.

"That's fair," she said.

"I, however, do have execute authority?" Jacob asked with a raised eyebrow.

"Just don't kill him," Saul said.

Out Processing
San Quentin State Prison
San Quentin, California
November 20, 1977

Susanne Bonafide stood beside her sedan with a bag full of fresh clothes in one hand and a cup of coffee in the other. Everyone thought she was out of her mind, including her fiancee Will Hessler. She wasn't sure if they were right or wrong, but she couldn't forget what she knew.

Specifically, she knew that Mary Gauss had changed. It had been a year of weekly visits to the prison, exactly fifty two of them. In the beginning Mary was vicious toward her, mocking her for being such a sap that she would think she could play a part in rehabilitating the woman who murdered her own father.

That lasted for several weeks, and then Mary realized Susanne would not give up, so the walls went up. The silent treatment lasted another few weeks, and then Mary broke down and begged Susanne to leave her alone.

That was when Susanne knew she was making a dent in the girl's hard shell. On some level Mary knew that what she had done was wrong. She didn't want the weekly reminders that Susanne represented. If she knew that she was wrong, that meant she could change. Just that single seedling of hope was enough for Susanne to keep pressing forward.

Then the conversations began, and by

month six they were actually beginning to develop what seemed to all observers to be a bizarre friendship.

Then the ACLU came calling. The circumstances of Mary's arrest (and specifically Inspector Ronald Stein punching her in the face) had caused an investigation to be opened by the State Attorney General. Both Susanne and Mary watched the news come in from week to week as the investigation proceeded until one day the news finally came.

She would be released.

They began making plans for her. She would move into a halfway house and begin attending City College again. Susanne had convinced the owner of a grocery store to hire her on as a bagger, at least in the beginning. With enough time she could work her way up.

Mary expressed concerns that her friendship with Susanne would end, but Susanne did her best to assuage her fears.

"People who have been through what we have been through together, that bond doesn't break easily."

.   .   .

"I can't believe I'm really out," Mary said with a smile. "I felt like I was in there forever."

"Well, it's over now," Susanne said. "And you won't ever have to go back there again."

Mary's face changed.

"If I can stay on the straight and narrow."

"That's the deal," Susanne confirmed. "I mean... you know that no one was happy about the ACLU getting your conviction overturned. There are many people waiting for you to fail."

"But not you," Mary said. "I still don't understand."

"Why I don't hate you?" Susanne asked.

"I guess maybe that's what makes us different."

"I've seen a lot of people let themselves be chewed up by hate, Mary. I'll be honest, it isn't easy but I'm just not willing to go down that road."

"I'm sorry," Mary said. "But I drank a bunch of water before they checked me out. I think there's a rest stop ahead, can we stop there?"

Susanne sat in the parking lot of the rest stop

and stared out at the mountains of the San Francisco north bay. It was a peaceful moment, and she hadn't known many of those in quite a while.

Was she doing the right thing? Did she really believe what she had told Mary? If she was being honest with herself, she wasn't sure. All she knew was that she wanted to be the person she was pretending to be. She wanted to be the person who believed that even a woman like Mary Gauss could change, and that even after all she had done, Susanne could forgive her.

Susanne heard the metal "clank" of the restroom door and turned to see Mary walking toward the car. That was strange. She was carrying a paper bag. Susanne searched her memory. Had Mary been carrying that bag when she went into the restroom?

An alarm went off somewhere deep in her brain and she felt a chill race down her spine.

Susanne moved fast, keying the engine and reaching for the shifter, but she was too late. Mary had dropped the paper bag and was now holding a pistol on her.

"Don't do anything stupid!" Mary snapped. "And you might just live through this."

The story continues in
Jericho Black Book Two: Kill Chain

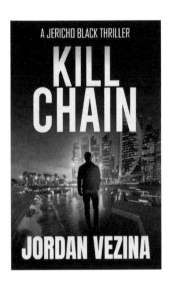

 **Jordan Vezina** is a fiction writer living in Northern California with his wife Emily Vezina where they run a business together. Jordan served in both the Marine Corps and Army Infantry, which gave him the background to develop many of the military based characters in the Jericho Black and Jack Bonafide series of books.

Copious research has always been an essential part of Jordan's writing process, so that books like Hard Red Winter and Among Wolves would be historically accurate and immerse the reader in the timeframe as well as the lives of the characters.

jordanvezina.com
me@jordanvezina.com

Printed in Great Britain
by Amazon